Early Field Recordings

An Edison spring-driven cylinder recorder/player of a type
commonly used by field researchers.

Photograph by Verlon Stone.

Early Field Recordings

A Catalogue of Cylinder Collections
at the Indiana University
Archives of Traditional Music

Edited by *Anthony Seeger*
and Louise S. Spear

Indiana University Press
Bloomington and Indianapolis

Library of Congress Cataloging-in-Publication Data

Indiana University, Bloomington. Archives of
  Traditional Music.
  Early field recordings.

  Bibliography: p.
  Includes indexes.
1. Phonocylinders—Indiana—Bloomington—Catalogs.
2. Indiana University, Bloomington. Archives of Traditional
  Music—Catalogs. I. Seeger, Anthony. II. Spear, Louise S.
ML156.2.I54 1987   016.7899'12   86-46030
ISBN 0-253-31840-8

1   2   3   4   5   91   90   89   88   87

*Dedicated to all the performers
recorded in these collections,
and to those who recorded them.*

Contents

Acknowledgments

This catalogue of the historic collections of field recordings on wax cylinders located at the Indiana University Archives of Traditional Music is based on the hard work and dedication of a large number of people and institutions. It involved many individuals who collaborated in cleaning and copying the nearly 7,000 cylinders, and many others who participated in the lengthly process of turning work sheets into a database and then into this catalogue. The considerable difficulties of the endeavor were compounded by the sheer size of the collections and the conflicting information about many of the individual items.

The Re-recording Project

The re-recording of the wax cylinders onto high quality magnetic tape was funded by the National Science Foundation, division of Systematic Anthropological Collections (BNS 83-9628). Directed by the editors, the recording project began in 1983 and was concluded in 1985. The project involved washing nearly 7,000 cylinders, repairing as many as possible, recording them onto magnetic tape, examining and whenever possible improving the documentation on each of the 158 collections, repacking them into acid-free cylinder boxes and placing those in new cardboard master boxes. Among those who helped the editors to plan the project and to begin the work were Nancy Cassell, Sally Childs-Helton, Bruce Harrah-Conforth, and Carol Inman. Erika Brady and Dorothy Sara Lee, of the Library of Congress Federal Cylinder Project, provided valuable suggestions about how to proceed. Nancy Cassell, Bruce Harrah-Conforth, Cornelia Fales, Catherine Foy, Michael Largey, Tom Passananti, Glenn Simonelli, William Wheeler and Marjorie Weiler were largely responsible for the recording aspects and for checking primary documentation against the sound recordings.

The Database and Catalogue

It took a vast amount of coding, cross-checking, and editing to turn the documentation of 10,000 items on 7,000 cylinders into a suitable database and to use the database to produce this catalogue. Sally Childs-Helton, Carol Inman, Ann Lentz, Glenn Simonelli, and Marjorie Weiler were largely responsible for researching and checking documentation against text sources in Archives files and elsewhere, and for coding computer input from the vast amount of information to be found there. Wallace Hooper was responsible for the construction of the database and for the mechanics of the production of the catalogue copy. With Linda Buescher, Carmen Calnan, Craig Watson, and Brenda Wilson, he corrected successive versions of the database and catalogue. Marilyn Graf, Carol Inman, and Glenn Simonelli solved the more difficult coding and cross-checking problems. Nancy Cassell, Ronald Engard, Wallace Hooper, Carol Inman, Ann Schertz, Glenn Simonelli, and Lisa Woble read the database proofs.

Nancy Cassell and Marilyn Graf wrote the descriptive paragraph for each collection using the original documentation. Marilyn Graf enhanced and corrected catalogue resources by drawing upon data and interpretations provided by the cylinder project collaborators, upon newly available manuscript sources from the estate of the late George Herzog, and upon her own extensive knowledge of the materials derived from the sixteen years she has worked with them.

Mary Russell and Brenda Nelson prepared authority files for coding and proof-reading. Brenda Nelson prepared the indices with proof-reading assistance from Karen Gahagan and Susan Richardson.

The editors are grateful to all of the many individuals and institutions involved in this project for their contributions. It is relatively easy to obtain and to store collections. To preserve them and make them available to the public requires a variety of skills, experience, and resources that are abundantly possessed by the individuals listed above. Without them the cylinders would still be sitting on the shelves, and this catalogue would never have become a reality.

How to Use This Catalogue

The object of this catalogue is to describe the unique early recordings at the Archives of Traditional Music and to provide access to the rare music and linguistic material recorded on them. All of the collections have been transfered onto magnetic tape, and copies are available for consultation, within the restrictions placed on the use of the collections described below.

This catalogue has three parts. The first part summarizes the importance of the collections and some of the challenges they presented to the members of the project who re-recorded them and produced the data for this catalogue. The second part lists the collections in order by Archives of Traditional Music accession number. In addition to location and size, a short paragraph describes some of the most important features of each collection. The information the Archives staff used in preparing these paragraphs came from a variety of sources, including inscriptions on the cylinder boxes or slips of paper inside them, indices provided by the institutions that deposited the collections or prepared by past Archives staff, field notes and correspondence found among the papers of the late George Herzog, publications, interviews, and other sources. The third part consists of four indices that may be used to locate specific information within the collections--by geographic name, by individuals' names, by culture group, and by subject.

This catalogue does not offer information about each cylinder, but rather about each collection of cylinders. Space, time, and often a lack of precise information prevented this. The Archives of Traditional Music will, however, provide photocopies copies of cylinder-by-cylinder information about specific collections on request.

The first part of the catalogue is written in narrative form, and is mainly important for those who know little

about wax cylinders, the recording process, or the way in
which the sounds have been preserved. It is largely self-
explanatory.

   The list of collections by their Archives number
requires more explanation, since each entry condenses a
fairly large amount of information. An example from the
catalogue will help. The numbers in {} brackets after
each item refer to explanations given below.

54-007-F. {1}   Wilfrid Dyson Hambly {2}, 1929-1930. {3}
    Angola[?] {4} [Zaire] {5}
      Mbundu {6} (African People) {7}
        Ingende {8}
          Prayers; speeches, addresses, etc.; Stories,
          narratives and anecdotes {9}
        Unknown Locations {10}
          Basket songs; Drum music; Speeches, addresses,
          etc.; Stories, narratives, and anecdotes; Unknown
          subjects {11}; Vocabulary and pronunciation

Number of Cylinders: 40 {12}
Number of Strips :   53 {13}
Sound Quality of Strips {14}:   F 17, P 14, VP 8, B 13, U 1.
Degree of Restriction {15}:   2

   This is an incomplete collection of.... {16}.

1. 54-007-F, accession number. This number is the unique
identification number the Archives of Traditional Music
has assigned to the collection. A "collection" of
cylinders is usually a number of cylinders that was
recorded or deposited as a group, for which there is
documentation indicating some kind of unity. The
cylinders may have been recorded in the same region, at
the same time, or by the same person, but this is not
always the case. The Archives, however, treats each
collection as a unit. A reader desiring further
information about any collection should always refer to
this number when writing or telephoning the Archives. The
number 54 means the collection was deposited prior to 1954
in the Archives; the number 007 indicates it was the
seventh one catalogued that year, and the letter F
indicates that this is a field-recorded collection, not a
commercial release. The Archives uses similar number
sequences for all its acquisitions.

2. The name or names of the collector(s) are given after
the identifying number. We almost always know the name of
the collector. When a collector's name is not known,
square brackets indicate the opinion of the Archives
staff.

3. The dates refer to the year(s) when the recordings were made. These recordings were made by Wilfrid Dyson Hambly in 1929-30. Sometimes there are two or more dates, usually indicating different field trips.

4. The country in which the recordings were made is always indented three spaces from the accession number. We have used the 1986 names for the countries, rather than the names they were known by at the time the recordings were made, because many of them have become independent nations.

5. Square brackets indicate the opinion of the Archives staff, as distinct from that found in earlier documentation. The Archives' policy is to separate our own surmises from the documentation that existed for the collections. Whenever square brackets appear, it expresses an opinion of the staff in 1986, and it is subject to change. For example, when we are quite certain the recordings were made in another country, we indicate this with square brackets; when there is doubt about the actual recording location--as in this example--we indicate this with square brackets and a question mark. In this collection, the staff thought the recordings were made in Zaire, on the basis of the written records that accompany the collection. Specialists in the region may eventually resolve our doubts. We welcome more exact information whenever possible, and will use it to update our files and database.

6. The name of the people or culture group is indented two spaces from the name of the country in which they were residing. In order to maintain consistency, we have used the name or spelling from either the Library of Congress Subject Headings (9th Edition) or the Human Relations Area Files Outline of World Cultures, 5th Edition. These are not necessarily the names the groups call themselves today, but they are the currently accepted way for listing them in bibliographies. In some cases we have distinguished the culture group of the item performed from the culture group of the performer or informant, indicated by (item) and (inf.) respectively. This was found to be necessary because of the frequency with which a Native American group may sing songs of other Native American groups. An example is 54-031-F, where Kiowa Indians sing a Wichita healing song.

7. To clarify the group name, the Library of Congress often adds a qualifier in brackets to distinguish the local name from similarly named culture groups.

8. The locality in which the recording was made. Ingende is a place in Zaire where the Mbundu live. The Archives staff has not always been able to verify the existence or spelling of these locations, and in those cases they are usually given as the collector has written them.

9. A list of the subjects recorded is indented a further
two spaces beneath the local geographical name. This list
is taken from the collector's documentation, and is meant
only to provide a general idea of the collection's
contents. No attempt has been made to define the genres;
most of the languages and cultures are unknown to the
Archives staff, and we have only provided general
designations. Upon request, the Archives of Traditional
music can supply information about individual collections
that provides more detailed information about each
cylinder.

10. Additional countries, people, or locations. If the
collection contains recordings from more than one country,
people, or location, these are listed consecutively
beneath the accession number. Because of the
indentations, it is easy to scan the collections by these
geographic and cultural identifications, and then to look
for the subjects for each local area.

11. The word "unknown" is used in a very specific way
throughout the catalogue: it means that the documentation
for the cylinder does not specify the information
required. The Archives staff has tried to avoid guessing;
when we believe we know where the origin was, we have
indicated that within square brackets. "Unknown" should
not be taken to indicate that the cylinders are completely
mysterious (although some are); it simply means that the
particular information required is not explicitly stated
anywhere.

12. Number of cylinders. This indicates how many
cylinders are in a collection.

13. Number of strips recorded. Collectors often recorded
more than one example on a cylinder. This was especially
common with the longer Dictaphone cylinders that could
record six minutes or more. Since the number of cylinders
does not give an accurate idea of the number of separate
items in the collection, we have also listed the total
number of strips in the entire collection.

14. Sound Quality of Strips. In evaluating the sound
quality, the Archives staff used as the criterion our
estimate of the ease with which a researcher could
transcribe the recording. The codes used are as follows:
                E = Excellent
                G = Good
                F = Fair
                P = Poor
                VP = Very Poor
                U = Unplayable
                B = Broken and Unplayable
                NR = Not Recorded
Cylinders or strips marked "excellent" provide clear and
distinct reproductions of the original performance, and

are free of most of the extraneous noises of wear and tear
that accumulate over the years. Lower ratings may
indicate that the collector's recording technique was
inadequate and that the performance was never properly
recorded, or it may be the result of frequent playing or
damage. "Good" cylinders and strips provide relatively
clear reproductions of the original performances, and
researchers should not have to contend with intrusive
levels of background noise. "Fair" cylinders and strips
may have high levels of surface noise, distortion, and
tracking problems, but the original performances are
audible. Transcription should be possible, but
researchers may have to listen carefully to follow the
performance. "Poor" and "very poor" sound quality
indicate that the original performances are partially or
completely obscured. Partial transcriptions may be
possible on these cylinders, but complete transcriptions
may be very difficult or impossible to achieve. Some
cylinders were so badly warped or cracked that they were
unplayable; others were broken beyond easy repair and were
not played. In a few cases, where multiple cylinder
copies had been made from the same original recording, we
did not copy all of the identical cylinders, indicated by
the letters NR for "not recorded."

15. Degree of Restriction. The use of every field
collection deposited in the Archives of Traditional Music
is governed by a contract with the depositor. The
contract apportions rights to the depositor, the Archives,
and the patron. There are three levels of access,
indicated by the numbers 1, 2, or 3, in this entry. The
rights of users under these options are given below:

    Option 1. The Archives controls the access to
    the collection. The Archives allows free
    scholarly use of the materials at its facilities
    in Bloomington, and supplies copies at cost to
    institutions and researchers.

    Option 2. Patrons may come to the Archives of
    Traditional Music and listen to the tapes.
    Institutions and researchers may obtain copies
    for personal research at cost. If they wish to
    use the recordings in records, broadcasts,
    telecasts, film, or other commercial means of
    dissemination, they must first obtain the
    authorization of the depositing individual or
    institution. The Archives will supply the name
    and address of the institution to the patron, who
    must obtain written authorization for any
    commercial use of the materials.

    Option 3. Patrons may come to the Archives and
    listen to the tapes, but they may not transcribe
    them or cite them extensively without the written
    authorization of the depositor. The Archives

will supply the name and address of the
institution to the patron, who must obtain
written authorization for any other use of the
materials.

16. Summary paragraph. This brief paragraph summarizes
some of the information the Archives has gathered about
the collection from a variety of sources. An attempt has
been made to indicate whether the collection is complete,
how good the documentation is for the collection (how
detailed the notes about each cylinder may be expected to
be), and a very brief indication of the contents. When a
few performers appear on many strips, their names are
listed if we have them, especially when these were
principal informants of the researchers. When we are
aware of a publication that discusses the collection, we
have included a reference. These summary paragraphs
sometimes mention specific cylinders, with a number in
brackets. The cylinders in the Archives have been given
consecutive numbers; the prefix LCY indicates a six-inch
long Dictaphone cylinder, while SCY indicates a four-inch
cylinder. These are used largely to identify cylinders
within collections. We also have a concordance for most
collections that allows us to translate the original
collector's numbers (often given in publications) into the
Archives number. The Archives usually has more
information about a collection than this paragraph
contains, and those interested should write or telephone
for more complete information on specific collections.

Using the Indices

   When patrons consult the Archives about collections,
they are usually interested in collections made by a
certain person, or recorded in a certain region, or
obtained from a certain culture group, or of a particular
subject. The four indices in this volume provide this
information about the cylinder collections.

Index of Geographical Areas is an alphabetical list of
countries and locations within countries in which
recordings were made. It is organized by continent or
large geographic region. For example, Zaire is found
under the heading Africa, and Ingende is listed under
Zaire. Because of the large number of collections
recorded there, the United States of America has been
further subdivided into states, and Canada has been
subdivided into provinces, both of them being found under
North America.

Index of Names gives the names of collectors and principal
performers. Performers names are only given when they
appear on a number of different cylinders. Some names of
expeditions or expositions have been included as well, for

example the second Wanamaker Historical Expedition on
which several collections were recorded has a heading of
its own.

Index of Culture Groups lists the names of the groups
recorded. The primary listing is always under the Library
of Congress Subject Heading (9th Edition) or the name
found the Human Relations Area File Outline of World
Cultures, 5th Edition. Alternative spellings we have come
across are given, as well as cross-refences from the
alternative names for some of the groups. Many of these
direct the user to a different heading. Thus "Blackfoot"
will say "see Siksika." The culture group index will also
refer readers to collections where members of one group
sing another group's songs; if the culture group is either
the performer, or the originator of what is performed, its
name will appear for a collection. When an alternative
name is next in the alphabetical order, we have placed it
in brackets after the previous one, in order to conserve
space (for example, Arapaho Indians {Arapahoe}).

Index of Subjects lists the major categories of speech and
music found in the collections, subdivided by culture
group. The categories are quite general, and are only
meant to lead the reader to the appropriate collection.
More detailed itemization of the contents of each cylinder
in a collection is available from the Archives upon
request. Collectors of Native American materials often
distinguished between "dance songs" (probably parts of
ceremonies) and "songs." We have followed the original
collectors' distinctions, but cannot be sure of the
difference for each collection.

How Obtain Further Information and Copies

   The recordings and documentation in the Archives of
Traditional Music are preserved for the use of interested
patrons, within the limits set by the contracts signed
with depositors, observing ethical considerations, and
with the understanding that whoever uses the materials
will give full credit to the original collector and
depositing institution, following standard academic
practice.

   When individuals or institutions desire further
information about a collection or several collections,
they should write to the Archives at the following
address:

                   Archives of Traditional Music
                        Morrison Hall
                      Indiana University
                   Bloomington, Indiana 47405

The letter should indicate the desire for further
information or for copies of the collection, give the
accession number(s) of the collection(s), and describe the
intended use of the recordings. The Archives staff will
respond to the request as swiftly as possible. If patrons
wish to telephone, they are encouraged to do so after
sending a letter, which allows the staff time to determine
the answers to the questions. There is a modest charge
for photocopying, and a variety of charges for making tape
copies, depending on the kind of tape, speed, format, and
special requirements. The Archives telephone number is
(812) 335-8632 for the offices, and (812) 335-8631 for the
library (as of 1986).

   If the collection is Option 2 or Option 3, the Archives
will provide the address of the depositor. It is the
responsibility of the patron to obtain the necessary
written authorization for the use he or she intends ot
make of the materials. All patrons will be required to
pay for photocopying and audio reproduction costs. They
will also be asked to sign a standard form indicating that
the copies are for scholarly or personal use, and will not
be copied or used for commercial purposes without prior
authorization.

   The Archives endeavors to process orders quickly, but
cannot guarantee an immediate response to a request for a
copy. It is important for patrons to plan ahead and
anticipate their need for a collection well in advance of
the date it should be delivered. The orders are filled as
soon as the staff is able to do so.

   This catalogue has been designed to make the unique
recordings at the Archives of Traditional Music more
widely known and more easily available to researchers.
The specific nature of these early and valuable recordings
required a different approach from most catalogues, and we
believe that the result should facilitate research and
stimulate the use of the materials that so many major
figures in the history of anthropology, linguistics, and
ethnomusicology recorded and that the Archives has
preserved.

Early Field Recordings

Ethnographic Cylinder Recordings
An Introduction[1]

The invention of the cylinder recorder in 1877 by Thomas Edison, and rapid improvements on the machine made in subsequent decades[2] were extremely important to the development of linguistics, anthropology, and ethnomusicology. For the first time, music and speech could be captured and preserved without relying on the collector's subjective transcriptions or memory. Before the invention of sound recording, collectors either summarized what they heard or asked the performer to repeat the same thing over and over while they tediously wrote down the text or sketched out the melody. When a song or myth could be recorded on a wax cylinder, it could be played back with relative accuracy and objectivity--at least until the cylinder ran out. Pitch, rhythm, pronunciation, inflection, style, and expression could be recorded simultaneously in a a manner impossible in written transcriptions. The cylinder recordings could be played repeatedly for the purposes of transcription and analysis by specialists far from the performance. Contemporary scientists were quick to see the usefulness of the cylinder recorder, and began to use it soon after its invention.

Recordings of non-Western music were made at the 1893 World's Columbian Exposition. In 1890 the first collection of Native American field recordings was made of the Passamaquoddy Indians in Maine by Jesse Walter Fewkes of Harvard. The subsequent analyses of these recordings fueled important theoretical debates in the entire

---

1. Some of the material in this section was delivered as papers and appeared in The Proceedings of the International Symposium on B. Pilsudski's Phonographic Records and the Ainu Culture, Hokkaido University, Sapporo, Japan. Pp. 39-54, and 101-107. The authors are grateful for authorization to use the material here.
2. The history of the phonograph industry is described in detail in Read and Welch (1959).

discipline. Edison machines were soon being carted off to
distant parts of the globe. In retrospect the invention
of the cylinder recorder is seen as central to the
successful study of oral traditions. Béla Bartók stated
in 1937, "I most definitely maintain that the science of
musical folklore has Edison to thank for its present
state of development." Jaap Kunst wrote, "Ethnomusicology
could never have grown into an independent science if the
gramaphone had not been invented. Only then was it
possible to record the musical expressions of a people
objectively" (1959:12).

Today, one hundred years after the first ethnographic
recordings, the voices of ethnographers and performers
long dead may still be discerned behind a veil of surface
hiss and noise, and the sounds preserved on the cylinders
continue to be important to scholars and descendents of
the performers.

The Indiana University Archives of Traditional Music in
Bloomington, Indiana, has one of the world's largest and
finest collections of ethnographic cylinder recordings.
The cylinders were recorded between 1893 and 1938 by
linguists, comparative musicologists, ethnographers, and
explorers. Other major collections are located at the
Archive of Folk Culture at the Library of Congress in
Washington, D.C., the Robert Lowie Museum at the
University of California at Berkeley, and at major sound
archives around the world.[3] The 6,985 cylinders in the
Archives of Traditional Music are only part of a far
larger collection of music and oral data from around the
world preserved on discs, wires, and magnetic tape, but
because of their age the cylinders are especially valuable
documents of traditions from over 150 different groups in
Africa, Black America, Native America, Asia, Europe and
Oceania.

The most important legacy from the early cylinder
recordings is the preservation of musical traditions,
languages, and narratives as they were performed
generations ago. Oral traditions are always changing, and
the wax cylinders provide the earliest accurate documents
of what traditions sounded like. In spite of their
relatively poor sound quality for those accustomed to
digital discs and today's high fidelity equipment, the wax
cylinders of the Archives of Traditional Music are
valuable documents. They have been used by a variety of
researchers in the past, and with this catalogue we expect
they will be even more useful in the future. Newly
independent nations frequently request copies of the
cylinders to house in their capital cities in order to
reconstruct their pre-colonial heritage. Native North
American groups interested in their cultural history have

---

3. Information on many of the early collections has been
summarized in Gillis 1984.

come to the Archives to learn, or re-learn, the languages
and songs of their ancestors by listening to tape copies
of the original cylinders. This catalogue should help
those interested in learning about what is preserved on
the wax cylinders in the Archives of Traditional Music.

The Provenance of the Wax Cylinder Collections

Many of the cylinder collections in the Archives of
Traditional Music were recorded on scientific expeditions
sponsored by major ethnographic museums, such as the
American Museum of Natural History in New York City, the
Field Museum of Natural History in Chicago, and the
University Museum of the University of Pennsylvania. The
recordings were sometimes only parts of larger collections
of artifacts assembled for the museums. Over the past
forty years, the Archives of Traditional Music has slowly
assembled the collections because it is an institution
specialized in the preservation of sound recordings.

Behind nearly every collection lies a tale of adventure
and a testimony to the dedication of the collectors. An
example is the collection of 136 cylinders recorded by
Waldemar Bogoras and Waldemar Jochelson in Siberia between
1900 and 1902 (54-149-F). Bogoras and Jochelson were
Russian researchers who, as very young men, were banished
to Siberia because of their revolutionary activities.
The two men were not confined, but were able to spend
their time in Siberia traveling and studying the various
peoples who lived there. The American Museum of Natural
History invited Bogoras and Jochelson to participate in
the Jesup North Pacific Expedition of 1901-1905. The aim
of the expedition was to explore the cultural connections
between the northwest coast of North America (Alaska) and
the northeast corner of Asia (Siberia).

Despite many physical hardships, Bogoras and Jochelson
recorded cylinders, took hundreds of photographs, took
physical measurements, made plaster casts of faces, and
collected museum objects, including a mammoth tusk
weighing 220 pounds. The cylinders include tales, shaman
songs, and other songs of the Arian Eskimos, Chukchi,
Koryaks, Tunguses, Yakuts, and Yukaghirs.[4]

The scientists encountered some difficult recording
situations. In his monograph The Chuckchee, Bogoras
describes recording ventriloquism, or "separate voices" on

---

4. In 1909-11 Jochelson collected Aleut cylinders in
Alaska. These were housed in the Fonogramarkhiv in
Leningrad. With the help of the Michael Krauss, of the
Alaska Native Language Center, the Archives of Traditional
Music and the Fonogramarkhiv exchanged copies of the Aleut
and Siberian recordings.

a cylinder:

> I tried to make a phonographic record of the
> "separate voices" of the "spirits." For this
> purpose I induced the shaman Scratching-Woman to
> give a seance in my house, overcoming his
> reluctance with a few extra presents. The
> performance, of course, had to be carried out in
> utter darkness: and I arranged my machine so as
> to be able to work it without any light.
> Scratching-Woman sat in the farthest corner of
> the spacious room, at a distance of twenty feet
> from me. When the light was put out, the
> "spirits," after some "bashful" hesitation,
> entered, in compliance with the demand of the
> shaman, and even began to talk into the funnel of
> the graphophone. The records show a very marked
> difference between the voice of the shaman
> himself, which sounds from afar, and the voices
> of the "spirits" who seemed to be talking
> directly into the funnel. (Bogoras 1975: 436).

Another early collection is a group of 64 cylinders
recorded by Captain George Comer in the Hudson Bay area of
Canada between 1903 and 1909. At the age of seventeen
Comer left his home in Connecticut for his first whaling
voyage. He became interested in the Eskimo people with
whom he came in contact, and in 1903 he was commissioned
by the Museum für Völkerkunde in Berlin and the
American Museum of Natural History in New York to obtain
clothing, charms, plaster casts of heads, hands, and feet,
recordings of songs, and notes on customs. Some of
Comer's journals have been edited by W. Gillies Ross and
published as An Arctic Whaling Diary: The Journal of
Captain George Comer in Hudson Bay, 1983-1905 (Ross 1984).
Among the cylinders is a song about Captain W.E. Parry and
his two ships, which sailed to the area in 1821 in search
of a northwest passage.[5]

Frederick Starr recorded cylinders in the Belgian Congo
(now Zaire) in 1906. Starr was an American anthropologist
whose research covered a number of countries, including
the United States, Mexico, the Philippines, Korea, and
Japan. While at the St. Louis Exposition, Starr met a
group of Africans from the Belgian Congo. This encouraged
him to travel there himself. He spent 53 weeks in Africa,
travelling some 8,000 miles and visiting 28 different
groups of Congolese. He returned with museum objects,
photographs, and 24 cylinder recordings. The cylinders
have been described by Frank J. Gillis (1968).

---

5. With the permission of the American Museum of Natural
History, The Archives of Traditional Music provided copies
of the cylinder recordings to Mr. Ross during his
research.

Many of the cylinder collections were recorded among Native American groups in the United States and Canada. James K. Dixon recorded cylinders of American Indians in the plains of Montana. In 1909 chiefs representing nearly every major Native American community in the United States gathered to present what was billed as the "Last Great Indian Council." Cylinders were recorded, photographs taken, and the Battle of the Little Big Horn was re-enacted for the motion picture cameras. The elaborate event was the second of three expeditions financed by Rodman Wanamaker, a son of John Wanamaker, who founded the successful Wanamaker department stores in Philadelphia and New York City. Dixon wrote about the Native American groups he visited in a book, The Vanishing Race: The Last Great Indian Council (1925). Photographs taken by Dixon can be found in American Indian Portraits from the Wanamaker Expedition of 1913 chosen and with an introduction by Charles R. Reynolds, Jr. (1971).

Not all the cylinder collections at the Archives of Traditional Music have been used for research, nor are they all as well documented as the ones described above. In some cases we are not even certain which group was recorded. But the possibility of matching the recordings to other descriptions of the events in publications, journals, and photographs greatly enriches the value of the sounds that have been preserved on the cylinders.

The Mechanics of Cylinder Recording

Cylinder recordings were made by literally inscribing sound waves into wax using a hard point fixed to the center of a flexible diaphragm at the end of a horn. It was done mechanically, without the use of electricity. Performers would talk, shout, or sing into the recording horn, which increased the force of the sound. The intensified sound waves would press on the diaphragm, and the hard point would cut more or less deeply into the wax. The spring driven recorder rotated the cylinder at between 80 and 200 times a minute. A tracking mechanism ensured that the stylus advanced steadily along the length of the cylinder--usually four or six inches--cutting approximately 100 grooves per inch.

To play back the cylinder, a somewhat lighter head with a needle affixed to the center of a diaphragm rides on the grooves as the cylinder rotates. The differences in the depth of the cuts in the wax produce vibrations in the diaphragm that, when amplified by a horn, reproduce the recorded sounds. Although the frequency response was relatively low by today's standards, the invention was immediately hailed as a tremendous technological breakthrough (amply described in Read and Welch 1959). The recording quality depended upon a combination of factors--

the nature and volume of the original sound, the physical
features of the recording horn, diaphragm, and cutting
device, and the quality of the wax itself. The best
remembered cylinders today are the hard, "Blue Amberol"
commercially issued cylinders, sold by the thousands. The
wax cylinders used for recording, however, were made of
softer wax. Since the playback heads were fairly heavy
and the wax was soft, repeated playing of a cylinder
destroyed the sound recorded on it. Some cylinders could
be recorded over and over by shaving them down
successively, which was as useful for research as for
office dictation and home entertainment. In spite of
their drawbacks, linguists and anthropologists continued
to use cylinder recorders long after cylinders had been
replaced by flat discs for commercial use because the
sturdy cylinder recorders required no electricity and were
well suited to field conditions.

   Recording conditions in the field were certainly far
from ideal. Jane Richardson Hanks described her
difficulties in a letter to George Herzog on October 8,
1938:

   The phonograph problem has become one of the
   sagas of the summer. (...) I had to get me a team
   and a demycrat (sic) to bring it down to the hall
   where I was to get the songs. However I set a
   date with a [man] and he arrived laden down with
   medicine articles to ensure a "correct version"
   of the songs. Alas, the night before, in setting
   up the machine, I found that Warburton, the Old
   Faithful of the Anthro[pology] Museum had failed
   to put into the box the crucial gadget: the
   recording diaphragm!! There was no time to head
   off my man, so I had to tell him to hold off the
   supernatural until I could conjure a gadget
   myself....

   [The recording diaphragm] arrived with a fanfare,
   and I sent a speeding horseman to my old man to
   call out the supernatural and come on over. The
   night before, though, I acted with more caution.
   I got an affable young man of 61 to sing a trial
   song, just to see that all was well. He sang. I
   looked, and you can imagine my emotions at
   looking at the cylinder and seeing, not a nice
   grove but a series of horrid gouges on the
   record! I examined the diaphragm, and it showed
   that the diamond was at the wrong angle or
   something. We tinkered but to no avail. Then
   mainly with the idea of making the Indians think
   I was doing something, I opened up the box to
   look at the insides, although I knew there was
   nothing wrong there. The supernatural through my
   guardian spirit took my hand and made me try to
   play the thing while the insides were all falling

out, and the box wide open. By Jove it made a
perfect groove! Tilting the diaphragm in that
way somehow shifted the weight so that it cut
perfectly. In a lather I bellowed into the horn
something that you will find on one of the
unnumbered cylinders....

So it came out all right, except that the horn
was vertical, making a devil of a position for
the singer who had to crook his neck over the
edge. Some I know are faint, but I only played a
part of 3 or 4 back, so they may be moderately
clear. Towards the end I think the singer
overblew. I shall be anxious to hear how they
came out. Each cylinder has the number scratched
onto it with a pin, usually at the wide end.
I'll send you shortly the notes that go with each
song. They are not as full as I hoped, for they
were taken, because of the above disasters, on
the last week of my stay.[6]

Many researchers could recount similar crises as they
battled with recalcitrant equipment in remote places
around the globe. The recordings eventually deposited in
archives have had a long, difficult, and varied history
that has affected their present sound. The cylinder
machines were durable, but recording problems, hard use,
and poor storage affected the sound quality of a number of
collections.

Copying wax cylinder recordings

In view of the fragility of the wax cylinders, many of
them had already been copied onto other cylinders, acetate
discs, or early magnetic tape for preservation purposes.
The 1983-85 project was the first to copy all the
cylinders, and the task presented the staff with complex
technical and ethnographic difficulties. The variety of
recording conditions, the fragility of the wax cylinders
themselves, and the passage of time all presented
challenges to the Archives staff who copied the cylinders
onto magnetic tape. The successful transfer of sound from
wax cylinders to modern magnetic tape requires more than
technological proficiency. The technician has to deal
with the deterioration of the wax, the characteristics of
the recording technology of the time, the way the
researchers used that technology, and the aesthetic values
of modern listeners. All of these affect the sound of the
recording, which may end up being quite different from the
original performance.

---

6. From a letter in the accession folder for 54-019-F;
used with the author's permission.

   The Archives has six original Edison cylinder players.
Each time a cylinder is played with these, however, the
heavy arm and needle further destroy the cylinder. The
sound quality worsens with each playing. Instead of using
the original machines, we borrowed a modern cylinder
player designed and constructed by Geoffrey Brown, of the
Lowie Museum at the University of California at Berkeley.
This machine had been used to copy the ethnographic
cylinders at the Lowie Museum and Library of Congress, and
it seemed well suited for our purposes. An original
Edison machine was used to play warped cylinders, or when
cracks caused the lighter arm of the modern machine to
skip grooves. The sound was transferred onto 1.5 mil
1/4-inch magnetic tape at 7.5 ips, using full track
configuration.

   We faced a number of challenges in the re-recording
process. These included (1) an ignorance of many of the
musical traditions involved, (2) damaged cylinders, (3)
unidentified recording processes, (4) irregular cylinder
velocity, and (5) inadequate documentation. For those who
plan to use the collections, it is useful to know about
these in order to interpret the sounds and the
documentation on them.

1. Unfamiliarity With the Tradition

   No individual can be familiar with all musical
traditions in the world. Since language and music vary
greatly from community to community, and within the same
community over time, it is dangerous to make any
judgements as to how a particular performance originally
sounded. When a sound technician uses filters to make the
sound more "agreeable" he or she is in fact interpreting
what the sound probably sounded like. We decided not to
use any filters, in order to preserve every trace that
remained of the original performance. This means that our
copies include the full gamut of sounds within the range
of sensitivity of the original cylinder. People using the
recordings must learn to listen for the meaningful sounds
behind a curtain of surface noise from the cylinder
itself. Should future researchers, familiar with a
particular tradition, wish to produce recordings that are
quieter, they will be able to do so. It is always
possible to delete certain types of sound later; it is not
possible to add them again once they have been taken away.
By filtering nothing out, we attempted to preserve all the
sounds for future use and experimentation.

   We also preseved the cylinders themselves for future
use. Laser cylinder players such as that developed at the
Institute of Applied Electricity of the University of
Hokkaido, Japan, and digital sound editing may permit
future technicians to obtain better sound from some of our

recordings than we were able to get with our limited
technology.[7] The cylinders have been stored in new acid-
free boxes and the climate control and fire security of
our facilities was improved to insure their survival into
the next century.

2. Restoring Damaged Cylinders

  Time has not been kind to the cylinders. They were
often collected for immediate transcription and were
subjected to extreme heat and cold when they were recorded
as well as later when they were placed in storage. The
most serious problem we encountered was mold, which could
appear in small spots or as a thick fuzzy growth. Mold
penetrates the wax itself, pitting or destroying the
grooves. We removed the mold by washing each cylinder
carefully in a mild solution of distilled water and the
detergent Joy. They were rinsed in a diluted mixture of
distilled water and a chemical Kodak Foto-Flo to prevent
water spots and then played when dry. Since the
collectors often indicated the contents of the cylinder on
the original cylinder boxes, we copied what they wrote
onto specially designed forms--a difficult procedure when
the handwriting was barely legible or the pencil faded by
the passage of decades. Just in case a problem of
interpretation were to arise in the future, all of the
original boxes on which there were markings were saved and
packed separately from the washed cylinders to avoid
recontaminating them with mold and dirt.

  Some of the cylinders were broken when we unpacked them.
The staff devised a practical approach when faced with
cylinder boxes full of pieces instead of an entire
cylinder. The first step in repairing a cylinder was to
piece together what was left of the wax, with sparing
application of quick-drying high-adhesive glue. Once the
pieces were fitted together, scraps of wax from blank
cylinders were melted down, and the soft wax applied to
the inside of the cylinder along the fracture. Then a
mask was cut, exposing an area just slightly larger than
the missing wax or fracture, and taped over the surface of
the cylinder so that only the broken area was exposed.
The melted wax was carefully applied to this area until it
covered the affected area. Using a sharp blade, the new
wax was gradually shaved down until level with the
original wax. Then new grooves were cut into the new wax
to match the old tracking. The result was usually a
playable cylinder where before there had been only pieces.
Since the cylinders revolve at a minimum of 80 rotations

---

  7. This process is described in Executive Committee of
the International Symposium, Hokkaido University, Sapporo
Japan (editors) 1985.

per minute, the patch of new wax is barely detectible.[8]

3. Setting the Speed

Cylinder recorders did not run at fixed speeds the way
modern tape recorders do. Instead, the speed varied from
model to model and machine to machine, and was more or
less easy to adjust on different models. Some researchers
slowed their machines down in order to be able to record
more on a cylinder, others recorded at whatever speed
their recorder operated at. Few sounded a tone at the
start of the recording. Whatever they did, they could
only estimate the number of rotations. This meant that
within a range of about 80 to 240 rotations per minute, it
was difficult to guess at the original recording speed.
Playing back a cylinder too slowly lowers the pitch, turns
a woman's voice into a man's, and can turn a rapid tune
into a slow march; playing it too fast can do the
reverse--speed a march to a jig, transform a man into a
woman, and raise the pitch of all the instruments
involved. Dealing with the variety of speeds encountered
on the wax cylinders was one of the most difficult
technical problems we encountered.

The modern cylinder player we used for copying was
easily adjusted for speed, which was indicated on a large
meter on the front of the machine. The problem remained,
however, of determining the original speed of the cylinder
recording. Decisions as to the speed had to be made by
people unfamiliar with the tradition. In collaboration
with Robert Port, of the Indiana University Linguistics
Department, we developed a system of determining the
correct speed of the cylinder on the basis of an
apparently universal articulation of the consonants K and
G. When the cylinder was in good enough condition that we
could clearly hear these consonants, we adjusted the speed
accordingly using them.

Given the relatively poor sound quality of many of the
cylinders, there will probably never be a satisfactory
solution to the problem of velocity, and thus of pitch.
People who use the cylinders in these collections should
not develop elaborate theories based on the absolute pitch
of the original performances. These are possibly not
accurately represented on our copies.

---

8. This description is taken from Harrah-Conforth
(1984). The use of a laser player has great advantages
when playing damaged cylinders, since the light can pass
right through a crack or even a hole in a cylinder and not
skip a groove.

4. Where the Medium Contains the Message

Sometimes the copying process produces sounds that were
not part of the original performance. This is obvious in
the case of the surface noise from the cylinder, but
sometimes it extends further. Many of the Native North
American recordings were of singers performing alone or
with a drum. Sometimes what sounded like a drum was not a
drum at all, but a crack in the cylinder. The close
examination of a recording which was described by earlier
technicians as "man sings with drum" showed that the drum-
like noise was produced by the thump of the needle hitting
a crack. Who knows what theories of Native American
rhythm could be developed using tapes that made cracks
sound like drums.[9] A similar misconception also resulted
when a patch of mold on one part of a cylinder produced a
sound interpreted as a rattle.

Other strange sounds resulted from the copying process.
After the initial copying was completed, we had a
different set of people make second copies and check the
originals for errors. They came across one example of a
man singing with whistle accompaniment. Strangely enough
there was no mention of whistling in the notes made by the
original ethnographer, although whistling is a common
practice for shamans in many regions. The sound was
explained on the next recording, when the technician could
be heard shouting to a friend that he wanted a pizza for
lunch. We deduced that the technician had forgotten to
turn the microphone off after his announcement, and that
his whistling had been recorded along with the sound of
the original cylinder. We copied the cylinder again,
without the whistle.

The use of noise suppression devices to eliminate the
hiss of the surface irregularities on the grooves can also
produce new sounds. When noise suppression was applied by
Japanese engineers to early recordings of the Ainu, the
resulting recording transformed some of the Ainu words
completely. Although the result was clearly much quieter,
the Ainu preferred to listen to the original where their
language was unchanged (Suzuki, 1985).

5. What is it?

Since many of the cylinder recordings were made by
ethnographers in the midst of their intensive studies of a
particular group, they did not always take great care to
document what they were recording. Researchers often find
the field experience so vivid at the time that they assume
they will remember when, where, and what they record.

_____

9. This is one reason we saved the original cylinders.

Later, when their collections find their way into museums
and later into archives, there is often little indication
of what was recorded and by whom. Sometimes there is
writing on the boxes, but that is not always a sure
indication of what is inside them. Wax cylinders were
sometimes shaved down and used again, yet the original
contents are still indicated on the box. Also, the
cylinders have sometimes been placed in incorrect boxes as
they were handled by different generations of
ethnographers, transcribers, and museum staff. The most
enduring identification of cylinders, as of field
recordings today, is when there are announcements at the
start of the recording. Such announcements are,
unfortunately, not found on every collection. The Archives
staff took great care to keep the cylinders from getting
mixed up in the washing, recording, and repacking process,
and we were even able to reunite some stray cylinders with
their original collections, but not in every case.

   Correct identification of a collection is like solving a
mystery. Clues may be discovered through familiarity with
the handwriting on the box, through experience with
different musical traditions, through the physical
characteristics of the cylinders (wax color, type of mold,
or inscriptions) and sometimes through fieldwork notebooks
and publications. In spite of our efforts, this catalogue
stands witness to a number of collections we know very
little about. We have preserved these, too, in the
anticipation that someday someone will be able to identify
them.

   The general lesson to be learned from this description
of the difficulties encountered by the Archives staff as
they copied the cylinder collections is that the
recording process involves various steps, each of which
can greatly effect the sounds on the tapes that are
eventually made available to the public. These
difficulties are not unique to the Archives of Traditional
Music, they confront archives and sound technicians
everywhere. Although the sounds have been preserved, some
sounds have been altered by physical deterioration and the
restoration process itself.

   The staff of the Archives of Traditional Music
endeavored to establish a constant standard for the
research, documentation, preservation, and re-recording of
the nearly 7,000 wax cylinders it holds. We are, however,
certain that we have not resolved the issues of sound
quality, cylinder velocity, or the identification of these
collections. We have, however, contributed significantly
to the preservation and dissemination of these unique
recordings; we have not destroyed any evidence that
already existed; and we are in a position to assist in
their distribution to interested individuals, groups, and
institutions. The entire process has been at once
challenging and humbling. Our work stands ready for the

constructive criticism that will lead to further advances
in our understanding and use of these unique sound
documents.

Bibliography Cited

Archives of Traditional Music, 1975. A Catalog of
    Phonorecordings of Music and Oral Data held by the
    Archives of Traditional Music. Boston: G. K. Hall and
    Company.

Bogoras, Waldemar, 1975. The Chuckchee. New York: AMS
    Press.

Cassell, Nancy, 1984. "Ethnographic Anomalies in Cylinder
    Recordings" in Resound, A Quarterly of the Archives of
    Traditional Music volume 3 number 4, pp. 5-6.

Dixon, Joseph K., 1925. The Vanishing Race: The Last
    Great Indian Council. Philadelphia: National American
    Indian Memorial Association Press, 1925.

Executive Committee of the International Symposium
    (editors) 1985. Proceedings of the International
    Symposium on B. Pilsudski's Phonographic Records and
    the Ainu Culture. Hokkaido University, Sapporo, Japan.

Gillis, Frank, 1968. "The Starr Collection of Recordings
    from the Congo (1906) in the Archives of Traditional
    Music, Indiana University" in Folklore and Folk Music
    Archivist Spring.

Gillis, Frank, 1984. "The Incunabula of Instantaneous
    Ethnomusicological Sound Recordings, 1890-1910: A
    Preliminary List" in J. Kassler and J. Stubington
    (eds.) Problems and Solutions: Occasional essays in
    musicology presented to Alice M. Moyle. Sydney: Hale
    and Iremonger, pp. 322-355.

Harrah-Conforth, Bruce, 1984. "Restoring the Past:
    Technical Developments in Cylinder Repair" in Resound:
    A Quarterly of the Archives of Traditional Music volume
    3 number 2, pp. 3-4.

Inman, Carol F., 1984. "The M.G. Chandler Collection: A
    Case Study for Reappraisal of Archival Materials" in
    Resound: A Quarterly of the Archives of Traditional
    Music volume 3 number 2 pp. 2-3.

Kunst, Jaap, 1959. Ethnomusicology: A study of its
    nature, its problems, methods and representative
    personalities to which is added a bibliography. Third
    Edition. The Hague: Martinus Nijhoff.

Lee, Dorothy Sara, 1979. Native North American Music and
    Oral Data: A Catalogue of Sound Recordings 1893-1976.
    Bloomington: Indiana University Press.

Reynolds, Charles R., Jr., 1971. American Indian
    Portraits from the Wanamaker Expedition of 1913.
    Brattleboro Vermont: The Stephen Green Press.

Ross, W. Gillies, 1984. An Arctic Whaling Diary: The
    Journal of Captain George Comer in Hudson Bay, 1903-
    1905. Toronto: University of Toronto Press.

Stone, Ruth M. and Frank Gillis (compilers) 1976. African
    Music and Oral Data: A Catalog of Field Recordings
    1902-1975. Bloomington: Indiana University Press.

Suzuki, J., 1985. "Enhancement of Speech Signal Embedded
    in Noise by SPAC (Speech Processing System by use of
    AutoCorrelation Function)" In Executive Committee of
    the Internatinal Symposium (editors) pp. 61-65.

Catalogue of Cylinder Collections

54-003-F. Robert H. Morey, 1935.
    Liberia or Sierra Leone
      Gbandi (African people)
        Unknown locations
          Unknown subjects
      Kuranko (African people)
        Unknown locations
          Unknown subjects
      Toma (African people)
        Unknown locations
          Dance songs; Unknown subjects; Warriors'songs
      Mandingo (African people)
        Unknown locations
          Laments; Love songs; Unknown subjects; War songs
      Unknown culture groups
        Unknown locations
          Humorous songs; Love songs; Society songs;
          Unknown subjects

Number of cylinders: 14
Number of strips: 16
Sound quality of strips: F 8,   P 3,   VP 3,   B 2.
Degree of restriction: 3

   This collection is incomplete; additional cylinders
recorded by Robert Morey are at the Eastman School of
Music, Rochester, New York. Much of the original
documentation for the collection, culled from cylinder box
inscriptions and from American Museum of Natural History
work notes, was found to be incomplete or illegible.
Genres are more thoroughly designated than any other
documentation field.

54-007-F. Wilfrid Dyson Hambly, 1929-1930.
    Angola[?] [Zaire]
      Mbundu (African people)
        Ingende

     Prayers; Speeches, addresses, etc.; Stories,
     narratives and anecdotes
  Unknown locations
     Basket songs; Drum music; Speeches, addresses,
     etc.; Stories, narratives and anecdotes; Unknown
     subjects; Vocabulary and pronunciation

Number of cylinders: 40
Number of strips: 53
Sound quality of strips: F 17, P 14, VP 8, B 13, U 1.
Degree of restriction: 2

   This is an incomplete collection of galvano-plastic
copies of copper electro-negatype cores, which are also
housed in the Archives of Traditional Music. Many of these
large cylinders have bad cracks, warps, and even exploded
ends, perhaps resulting from severe heat or water damage.
In some cases, only half of the cylinder is playable.
   Each cylinder contains a lengthy spoken announcement.
Whenever possible, these announcements have been
transcribed by the Cylinder Project technicians; the
transcriptions can be found in the collection's accession
folder. Some announcements document the difficulties of
early cylinder recording, as with "We will now try the
same story, but instead of speaking into the large funnel,
Ngonga will speak into the small funnel. I have asked him
to speak very slowly and to say each word distinctly. It
is necessary to shout loudly." (Cylinder SCY 0316) In some
cases, entire folktales have been translated, presumably
by Hambly, into English; the English version of the tale
precedes the Mbundu. Some cylinders sound like examples of
linguistic (grammatical) drills in the Mbundu language.
(Cylinder SCY 0333; 0342; 0343; 0352-0355).
   Hambly sometimes announces that he is making a recording
"at Ingende, near Lake Tumba, Angola." However, Ingende
is in Zaire and to the best of our knowledge has never
been part of Angola.

54-009-F. Mary Rosamond Haas and Morris Swadesh, 1933.
  United States
     Cherokee Indians
        Unknown locations
           Stories, narratives and anecdotes
     Natchez Indians
        Oklahoma, Gove
           Speeches, addresses, etc.; Stories, narratives
           and anecdotes; Unknown subjects
     Natchez Indians (inf.); Cherokee Indians (item)
        Unknown locations
           Unknown subjects
     Natchez Indians and Cherokee Indians
        Unknown locations
           Stories, narratives and anecdotes
     Tunica Indians
        Louisiana, Marksville

        Bear dance songs; Dance songs; Duck dance songs;
        Rabbit dance songs; Round dance songs; Stories,
        narratives and anecdotes (songs from); Unknown
        subjects
      Unknown locations
        Stories, narratives and anecdotes; Unknown
        subjects
    Unknown culture groups
      Unknown locations
        Stories, narratives and anecdotes; Unknown
        subjects

Number of cylinders: 55
Number of strips: 127
Sound quality of strips: F 114, P 13.
Degree of restriction: 3

   Wide variance in the original collector's numbers
strongly suggests that these cylinders do not make up a
complete collection. The culture groups represented
appear to be Cherokee, Natchez, and Tunica.
   All of the Tunica recordings are performed by the same
singer, Sam Young, of Marksville, Louisiana. He sometimes
appears as a solo singer, and sometimes is part of a group
of male singers. All of these Tunica songs are
accompanied by a percussion instrument. There are also a
few narrative recordings. One cylinder of this group, a
clear anomaly, seems to be a researcher's comments about
the sociological and psychological behavior of the
Indians. (Cylinder SCY 0655) This voice may be that of
Morris Swadesh.

54-010-F. George Amos Dorsey, 1899
    Canada
      Kwakiutl Indians
        British Columbia, Hope Island
          Bear dance songs; Chief's songs; Dance songs;
          Eagle dance songs; Peace songs; Potlatch songs;
          Sacred songs; Songs of honor and praise; Winter
          songs; Wolf dance songs

Number of cylinders: 7
Number of strips: 7
Sound quality of strips: G 2, F 2, P 3.
Degree of restriction: 2

   This is an incomplete collection, deficient in written
documentation. Fortunately, the spoken announcements on
the cylinders themselves provide some information. The
main informant is Tom Haimasela of Nawhitti, Hope Island,
a member of the group of Kwakiutl Indians who performed at
the World's Columbian Exposition of 1893 in Chicago.

54-011-F. George Amos Dorsey [?] and James R. Murie [?],
           [ca. 1902?].
    United States
      [Pawnee Indians?]
        Unknown locations
          Unknown subjects
        Unknown culture groups
          Unknown locations
            Unknown subjects

Number of cylinders: 18
Number of strips: 18
Sound quality of strips: G 5,   F 8,   P 3.
Degree of restriction: 2

   Wilfred Hambly assigned the identification numbers for
these cylinders at the Field Museum of Natural History in
Chicago. An additional 125 unnumbered cylinders were sent
to Columbia University, where they were also assigned
numbers and added to the previous Dorsey Pawnee materials.
The result of this diversity of numbering systems has been
a great deal of confusion. The cylinders in this
collection represent, largely, Pawnee recordings of
questionable origin.

54-013-F. Jaime de Angulo, 1925
    United States
      Achomawi Indians
        California
          Dance songs; Doctors' songs; Ghost dance songs;
          Loon songs; Medicine songs; Puberty rites;
          Puberty rites (female); Rat songs; Round dance
          songs; Speeches, addresses, etc.; Victory songs

Number of cylinders: 11
Number of strips: 22
Sound quality of strips: F 10,   P 8,   VP 4.
Degree of restriction: 1

   This incomplete collection was brought to Indiana
University by George Herzog. The first tape copies were
made in 1957.
   The documentation has gaps, as it has been culled only
from cylinder box inscriptions and accession folder work
notes for the 1957 recordings. Announcements on the
cylinders identify Dick Wawhee from German Lake and Dick
Dowington from Reno as performers.

54-014-F. Morris Edward Opler and Jules Henry, 1933.
    United States
      Mescalero Indians
        New Mexico
          Unknown subjects

Number of cylinders: 79
Number of strips: 175
Sound quality of strips: G 4,   F 99,   P 57,   VP 14,   U 1.
Degree of restriction: 3

   These cylinders were recorded during a Columbia
University field expedition, led by Ruth Benedict, to the
Mescalero Indian Reservation in New Mexico.
   Documentation for the collection is scant, and the
deteriorating effects of mold have reduced the volume of
some cylinders and added to the roar of surface noise.

54-017-F. Felix S. Cohen, ca. 1930.
   United States
      Assiniboin Indians
         Montana, Fort Belknap Indian Reservation
            Death songs; Grass dance songs; Love songs; Owl
            dance songs; Speeches, addresses, etc.; Sun dance
            songs; Warriors' songs; Winter songs

Number of cylinders: 6
Number of strips: 6
Sound quality of strips: F 6.
Degree of restriction: 1

   Clear announcements on the cylinders confirm the
accuracy of the written documentation, and provide the
names of the performers: Henry Chopwood, Simon
Firstshoot, Talks Different, Wing Gray and Rex Flying.

54-019-F. Jane Richardson Hanks, 1938-1939.
   Canada
      Siksika Indians
         Alberta, Gleichen, Blackfoot Indian Reservation
         Unknown subjects

Number of cylinders: 25
Number of strips: 34
Sound quality of strips: G 8,   F 16,   P 4,   VP 1,   U 5.
Degree of restriction: 3

   Jane Richardson Hanks began her study of the Siksika in
1938 as the only anthropologist and experienced field
worker among a group of researchers studying the social
psychology of the Northern Blackfoot. During the summer
of 1939, Dr. Hanks returned to the Alberta reservation to
participate in a study sponsored by Columbia University.
Dr. Hank's field notebooks for the 1938 field trip were
deposited at the National Museum of Man in Ottawa.

Reference:
Lucien M. Hanks, Jr. and Jane Richardson Hanks. Tribe
under Trust: A Study of the Blackfoot Reserve of Alberta,
Toronto: University of Toronto Press, 1950.

54-025-F. Felix S. Cohen, ca. 1930.
    United States
        Atsina Indians
            Montana, Fort Belknap Indian Reservation
                Society songs; Sun dance songs; Victory songs

Number of cylinders: 4
Number of strips: 4
Sound quality of strips: P 4.
Degree of restriction: 1

    This collection may be incomplete, as it contains only
four cylinders. Inscriptions on the boxes make up the
documentation source; there are no collector's notes and
no announcements on the recordings. The performers are
Thick and Ed Blackbird, Tom Badrobe, Charlie Arms, and
Sadie Croff.

54-027-F. Natalie Curtis Burlin, 1903.
    United States
        Hopi Indians
            Arizona, Oraibi
                Kachinas
            Unknown locations
                Antelope songs; Buffalo songs; Dance songs;
                Hunting songs; Invectives and derisions;
                Kachinas; Lullabies; Marriage rites and
                ceremonies; Personal songs; Owl songs; Rabbit
                songs; Rites and ceremonies[?]; Sacred songs;
                Scouts' songs; Snake songs; Song cycles;
                Speeches, addresses, etc.; Unknown subjects; War
                songs
        Hopi Indians [?]
            Unknown locations
                Unknown subjects

Number of cylinders: 61
Number of strips: 65
Sound quality of strips: F 53, P 9, B 3.
Degree of restriction: 2

    This collection came to the Archives from the Field
Museum of Natural History. A related collection, 54-118-F,
contains recordings of many of the same informants and
genres.
    Although the collector's numbers are consecutive for
these cylinders, they may not constitute a complete
collection, due to incomplete sections of the song cycles.
The documentation for the Burlin cylinders has been
gathered from cylinder box inscriptions.

Reference:
Natalie Curtis. The Indian's Book. New York: Dover
Publications, 1968.

54-028-F. William Nelson Fenton, 1933.
    United States
        Seneca Indians
            New York, Cold Springs, Allegany Reservation
                Corn dance songs; Dance songs; Devils' songs;
                Feather dance songs; Fish dance songs; Funeral
                rites and ceremonies; Healing songs; Marriage
                rites and ceremonies; Raccoon dance songs; Social
                dance songs; Society songs; Songs of thanks; Star
                songs; Unknown subjects; War dance songs; War
                songs; Women's dance songs

Number of cylinders: 40
Number of strips: 55
Sound quality of strips: G 26, F 18, P 10, B 1.
Degree of restriction: 3

   These cylinders represent the singing styles of more
than a dozen informants. The songs themselves are social
and ritual songs, often accompanied by drum or rattle.
   Documentation for the collection, which includes Seneca
Iroquois names for the individual songs, is supplemented
by Fenton's notes to the recordings and transcriptions of
the song texts. Each cylinder has a pitch (usually A,
440 beats per second), a useful indication of the
appropriate recording speed.

54-029-F. Frank Gouldsmith Speck and Alexander J.
           General, 1928.
    Canada
        Cayuga Indians
            Ontario, Six Nations Reserve, Brantford
                Crocodile dance songs; Dance songs; Duck dance
                songs; Feast songs; Fish dance songs; Medicine
                songs; Meeting songs; Pigeon dance songs;
                Planting songs; Rites and ceremonies; Social
                dance songs; Society songs; Songs for the dead;
                Songs of thanks; Sun dance songs; Warriors' dance
                songs; Women's dance songs; Women's songs
        Cayuga Indians (inf.); Chippewa Indians (item)
            Ontario, Six Nations Reserve, Brantford
                Songs of thanks
        Cayuga Indians (inf.); Delaware Indians (item)
            Ontario, Six Nations Reserve, Brantford
                Dance songs; Planting songs; Rites and
                ceremonies; Songs of thanks; Women's songs
        Cayuga Indians (inf.); Mohawk Indians (item)
            Ontario, Six Nations Reserve, Brantford
                Medicine songs; Rites and ceremonies
        Cayuga Indians (inf.); Tuscarora Indians (item)
            Ontario, Six Nations Reserve, Brantford
                Eagle dance songs; Women's dance songs
        Cayuga Indians (inf.); Tutelo Indians (item)
            Ontario, Six Nations Reserve, Brantford
                Fire dance songs; Planting songs; Rites and

        ceremonies; Thunder dance songs; War dance songs;
        Winter songs
    Unknown culture groups
        Ontario, Six Nations Reserve, Brantford
            Fish dance songs; Planting songs; Rites and
            ceremonies; Women's songs

Number of cylinders: 38
Number of strips: 77
Sound quality of strips: G 28, F 47, P 2.
Degree of restriction: 1

    Documentation for this collection was compiled from
transcriptions of announcements made on the cylinders,
notes found inside the original cylinder boxes, as well as
correspondence between Frank Speck, George Herzog, and
Alexander J. General. Herzog prepared music and text
transcriptions of a number of the recordings, and these
may be consulted as a part of the documentation. The
transcriptions were apparently prepared for a publication
on Cayuga midwinter ceremonies which Speck began in the
1930s. This work (Midwinter Rites of the Cayuga Long
House, Philadelphia: University of Pennsylvania Press) was
published in 1949 without transcriptions.
    Speck's principal informant, Alexander J. General (Chief
Deskáheh) recorded several of the cylinders in this
collection after Speck had left the field. Also of
interest is the fact that Frank Speck himself participates
as an informant, singing his imitation of a raccoon dance
song (LCY 0115, strip B).

54-031-F. Jane Richardson Hanks, 1935.
    United States
    Kiowa Indians
        Oklahoma, Anadarka or Carnegie
            Beaver songs; Boys' songs; Buffalo songs; Dance
            songs; Deer songs; Doctors' songs; Flute music;
            Flute songs; Hand game songs; Healing songs;
            Hunting songs; Lodge songs; Love songs; Morning
            songs; Mothers' songs; Peyote songs; Pipe songs;
            Prairie dog songs; Prayer songs; Round dance
            songs; Scalp dance songs; Society songs; Song
            cycles; Stories, narratives and anecdotes; Sun
            dance songs; Victory songs; War songs; Women's
            songs
    Kiowa Indians (inf.); Wichita Indians (item)
        Oklahoma, Anadarka or Carnegie
            Healing songs

Number of cylinders: 41
Number of strips: 154
Sound quality of strips: EX 9, G 89, F 41, P 15.
Degree of restriction: 3

    This complete collection of cylinders was recorded in

the summer of 1935 on an expedition sponsored by Santa
Fe's Laboratory of Anthropology. Dr.Hanks' detailed field
notes, including text translations of songs and sketches
of instruments, provide valuable documentation to the
recordings.
   The main informants are White Horse, Old Man Horse,
Monroe Hunting Horse, Bilo Cozad, and Stumbling Bear.

54-033-F. Leslie Spier, 1935.
     United States
       Klamath Indians
          Oregon
             Healing songs; Love songs; Scalp dance songs

Number of cylinders: 3
Number of strips: 7
Sound quality of strips: F 5, P 2.
Degree of restriction: 2

   The Archives of Traditional Music holds only three of
what was originally a group of thirty-six cylinders loaned
to George Herzog when he and Spier planned to collaborate
on a publication about the Klamath. The publication did
not materialize, and the majority of the cylinders were
returned to Spier.
   These few cylinders are unremarkable in contents or
quality. However, the Archives holds disc copies of
Spier's complete collection which were made while Herzog
was in charge of the Columbia University Archives of Folk
and Primitive Music. Leslie Spier's notes to the
recordings, found among the papers of George Herzog,
provide very useful documentation.

54-034-F. Erna Gunther, 1925.
     United States
       British Americans
          Washington, Jamestown
             Sacred songs
       Clallam Indians
          Washington, Jamestown
             Canoe songs; Dance songs; Gambling songs; Love
             songs; Puberty rites; Society songs; Spirit
             songs; Thunder songs; Unknown subjects; War songs

Number of cylinders: 18
Number of strips: 37
Sound quality of strips: G 2, F 13, P 8, VP 4, B 5,
        U 5.
Degree of restriction: 3

   Two informants, Joe Johnson and Robert Collier, perform
a great variety of songs. Some contextual information is
included in the song descriptions, as with "Jollying song
- men making fun of women."

   The following bibliographic citation may be of help to
researchers of this collection: Gunther, Erna. "Klallam
Ethnography," in University of Washington Publications in
Anthropology, Vol. I, Part 5.

54-035-F.   Franz Boas [and John Comfort Fillmore?],
            [1893?] and Julie Averkieva, 1930.
   Canada
     Kwakiutl Indians
        British Columbia, Vancouver Island, Fort Rupert
           Dance songs; Fish dance songs; Unknown subjects
   Canada[?]
     Kwakiutl Indians
        British Columbia, Vancouver Island, Fort Rupert[?]
           Unknown subjects
   United States [?]
     Kwakiutl Indians
        Illinois[?], Chicago
           Unknown subjects
   United States or Canada
     Kwakiutl Indians
        Unknown locations
           Children's songs; Feast songs; Game songs; Ghost
           songs; Laments; Love songs; Men's songs;
           Lullabies; Potlatch songs; Purification songs;
           Rites and ceremonies; Unknown subjects; War
           songs; Women's songs

Number of cylinders: 91
Number of strips: 102
Sound quality of strips: F 26,   P 66,   VP 7,   B 2,   U 1.
Degree of restriction: 2

   This collection and two other related collections (54-
121-F and 83-917-F) are plagued with unresolved issues in
documentation. Inscriptions on the cylinder boxes
referred to recordings made both in Chicago, at the
World's Columbian Exposition, and at Fort Rupert.
   Informants for these recordings are many, and the genres
are similarly varied. Many of the selections are
performed with a drum accompaniment.

54-039-F.   Gladys Amanda Reichard, ca. 1938.
   United States
     Navaho Indians
        Unknown locations
           Autumn songs; Dance songs; Death songs; Medicine
           songs[?]; Prayers; Rain songs; Unknown subjects
     Navaho Indians (item)
        Unknown locations
           Unknown subjects

Number of cylinders: 97
Number of strips: 230

Sound quality of strips: G 195, F 18, P 12, VP 2,
        B 1, U 2.
Degree of restriction: 1

   Despite this collection's size, it may not be complete.
Other than information gathered from occasional
announcements on the cylinder recordings or from
inscriptions on the original cylinder boxes, the
documentation for this collection is sparse. No
informants are named. The announcements are of song
descriptions only, as with "The next song accompanies the
drinking of the medicine of the second night." (LCY 0204,
strips C, D)

54-041-F. Edward Sapir, 1910, 1913-1914, and Morris
           Swadesh, 1931.
   Canada
     Americans
       Unknown locations
         Music, popular
     Americans (item)
       [British Columbia, Vancouver Island?]
         Unknown subjects
     Nitinat Indians
       [British Columbia, Vancouver Island ?]
         Music, Popular; Prayer songs; Stories, narratives
         and anecdotes; Unknown subjects
   United States
     Americans
       Unknown locations
         Music, Popular

Number of cylinders: 148
Number of strips: 244
Sound quality of strips: G 8, F 150, P 77, B 7, U 2.
Degree of restriction: 3

   This collection of recordings was deposited in the
Archives of Traditional Music by Mary R. Haas. Most of
the cylinders were recorded by Edward Sapir when he was
associated with the National Museum of Canada. These were
transcribed by Helen H. Roberts and Morris Swadesh and
published in Roberts and Swadesh, "Songs of the Nootka
Indians of Western Vancouver Island Based on Phonographic
Records, Linguistic and Other Field Notes made by Edward
Sapir," Transactions of the American Philosophical
Society, n.s., Vol. 45, part 3, June 1955.
   Transcriptions of the Swadesh recordings appear in (Haas
and Swadesh) "A Visit to the Other World: A Nitinat text,"
International Journal of American Linguistics, Vol. 7,
1933.
   The long cylinders in this collection are duplicate
copies of the small cylinders.

54-042-F. Ruth Murray Underhill, 1931 and 1933.
     United States
        Papago Indians
           Unknown locations
              Corn songs; Deer dance songs; Drinking songs;
              Feast songs; Festival songs; Girl's songs;
              Healing songs; Meeting songs[?]; Planting songs;
              Pubery rites (female); Purification songs; Rites
              and ceremonies; Shamans' songs; Speeches,
              addresses, etc.; Stories, narratives and
              anecdotes; Unknown subjects; Victory dance songs;
              War songs; Work songs[?]

Number of cylinders: 28
Number of strips: 230
Sound quality of strips: G 161, F 53, P 12, VP 3,
        B 1.
Degree of restriction: 2

    This collection appears to be complete. Although little
written documentation has been found for these cylinders,
they do contain spoken announcements, most of which have
been transcribed by the Cylinder Project technicians.
Each cylinder contains quite a few short songs; sometimes
as many as sixteen selections are sung on one record
(Cylinder SCY 0593).
    The informants are named: Santiago Maristo, Juan Diego,
Jose and Juan Pancho, Juan and Patricio Lopez.

54-043-F. Thelma Adamson, ca. 1930.
     United States
        Nooksack Indians (item)
           Washington
              Unknown subjects

Number of cylinders: 2
Number of strips: 3
Sound quality of strips: P 3.
Degree of restriction: 3

    Documentation for these cylinders consists of a place
name, culture group and music transcriptions prepared by
George Herzog for Adamson's publication, "Folk-Tales of
the Coast Salish," Memoirs of the American Folk-Lore
Society, vol. 22 (1934), pp. 422-430.

54-044-F. George Amos Dorsey and James R. Murie, 1902.
     United States
        [Arapaho Indians or Pawnee Indians]
           [Oklahoma, Pawnee?]
              Stories, narratives, and anecdotes; War songs
        Arikara Indians
           [Oklahoma, Pawnee?]
              Bear dance songs; Corn songs; Coyote songs; Dance

      songs; Doctors' songs; Drinking songs; Fox dance
      songs; Medicine bundle songs; Medicine songs;
      Rites and ceremonies; Round dance songs; Scalp
      dance songs; Snake songs; Songs of thanks; Star
      ceremonies; Stories, narratives and anecdotes;
      Unknown subjects; Victory songs; War dance songs;
      War songs; Women's dance songs; Women's songs
    Cheyenne Indians
      [Oklahoma, Pawnee?]
      Unknown subjects
    [Cheyenne Indians?]
      [Oklahoma, Pawnee?]
      Unknown subjects
    [Mandan?] Indians
      [Oklahoma, Pawnee?]
      Buffalo dance songs
    Pawnee Indians
      [Oklahoma, Pawnee?]
      Autumn songs; Buffalo songs; Corn ceremonies;
      Corn dance songs; Coyote songs; Crow dance songs;
      Dance songs; Ghost dance songs; Greeting songs;
      Hand dance songs; Lightning songs; Love songs;
      Medicine bundle songs; Men's songs; Name songs;
      Offering songs; Peyote songs; Pipe dance songs;
      Rites and ceremonies; Scalp dance songs; Scalp
      songs; Scouts' songs; Skull songs; Society songs;
      Songs of thanks; Speeches, addresses, etc.;
      Spring songs; Star ceremonies; Star songs;
      Stories, narratives and anecdotes; Sun dance
      songs; Thunder ceremonies; Unknown subjects;
      Victory songs; War songs; Warriors' songs; Winter
      songs; Women's dance songs; Women's songs
    Pawnee Indians[?]
      [Oklahoma, Pawnee?]
      Unknown subjects
    Unknown culture groups
      [Oklahoma, Pawnee?]
      Unknown subjects; Victory songs
    Wichita Indians
      [Oklahoma, Pawnee?]
      Name songs; Rites and ceremonies

Number of cylinders: 443
Number of strips: 443
Sound quality of strips: EX 2, G 84, F 167, P 147,
     VP 14, B 27, U 2.
Degree of restriction: 2

   Although large, this collection is not complete; missing
cylinders, previously uncatalogued recordings, and
misplaced cylinders have contributed to the
inconsistencies. Still, of the numerous cylinders
documented here, many are of great value to North American
Indian scholars. In some cases, the performer, the date
of the performance, and a detailed song title (e.g. "Corn
ceremony; Searching for plant (in) Spring") are given.

The scholar of this material will be encouraged by the
fact that there are substantial manuscripts which
supplement this collection. For example, nine hundred
pages of transcriptions of recordings of Pawnee songs by
Helen Roberts are presently housed in the National
Anthropological Archives of the Smithsonian Institution.
The Field Museum of Natural History, Chicago, also holds
transcriptions of Pawnee material, possibly done by Erich
M. von Hornbostel. An article about Dorsey's work among
the Pawnee may be found in the Journal of American
Folklore, Vol. 17-18 (1904), pp. 189-196.

54-045-F. George Amos Dorsey and Erich M. von Hornbostel,
           1906.
    United States
      Pawnee Indians
        Oklahoma, Pawnee
          Bear dance songs; Bear songs; Coyote songs; Fox
          songs; Ghost dance songs; Peyote songs; Unknown
          subjects
        Unknown locations
          Buffalo songs; Doctors' songs; Stories,
          narratives, and anecdotes (songs from); Unknown
          subjects
      [Pawnee Indians]
        Unknown locations
          Unknown subjects

Number of cylinders: 18
Number of strips: 18
Sound quality of strips: P 1,   VP 16,   B 1.
Degree of restriction: 2

    The historical background for these eighteen cylinders
is quite interesting: it seems that a field work
collaboration took place in 1906, in Oklahoma, involving
Erich von Hornbostel and George Dorsey. The collection
came to the Archives of Traditional Music from the Field
Museum of Natural History, arriving in boxes labelled
"Phonogram Archiv des Psycholog. Instituts der Universitat
Berlin." Some of the labels contained the name of Dorsey;
others were marked von Hornbostel.
    It is therefore most unfortunate that the sound quality
of the cylinders is consistently very poor.

54-047-F. George Amos Dorsey[?], 1906.
    [United States?]
      Chinese
        [Illinois, Chicago?]
          Theater music

Number of cylinders: 1
Number of strips: 1
Sound quality of strips: F 1.

Degree of restriction: 2

   This is a mystery cylinder; the only valid documentation
comes from an announcement on the recording itself,
identifying the material as being Chinese, performed by
the Jackson Street Theater Band.

54-051-F.   Alexander Lesser and Gene Weltfish, ca. 1930.
    United States
      Pawnee Indians
        Unknown locations
            Flute music; Love songs; Musical intervals and
            scales; Sacrificial offerings; Speeches,
            addresses, etc.; Unknown subjects
      Wichita Indians
        Unknown locations
            Rain songs

Number of cylinders: 11
Number of strips: 36
Sound quality of strips: G 28,   F 5,   VP 2,   U 1.
Degree of restriction: 3

   There are nine Pawnee and two Wichita cylinders in this
collection. One of the listed informants, Mark Everts,
also performed for ethnologists Frances Densmore and Mark
Ellison.
   One of the two flute performances seems to be a
methodical demonstration of the tones of the instrument.

54-052-F.   John Alden Mason, 1923.
    Colombia
      Arhuaco Indians
        Don Diego Arriba
            Rejoicing songs; Unknown subjects
        Palomino
            Unknown subjects; Women's songs
        Pueblo Viejo
            Flute music; Instrumental music
        San Andres
            Unknown subjects
        San Francisco
            Unknown subjects
        San Miguel
            Flute music; Healing songs
        Santa Rosa
            Love songs; Unknown subjects; Women's songs

Number of cylinders: 30
Number of strips: 53
Sound quality of strips: G 22,   F 25,   P 6.
Degree of restriction: 2

   This collection was originally deposited in the Field
Museum of Natural History in Chicago. Cylinder recordings
of South American Indian music are rare, so this
collection is especially valuable, as it seems to be
complete, and has survived with much of its documentation
in good order.
   Many of the Arhuaco cylinders contain spoken
announcements which, when audible, provide the name of the
song, the name of the singer, the location of the
recording, and the date.
   Some of the cylinders have been repaired and played for
the first time in many years. These are audible but the
sound is distorted by cracks and pops.
   This collection is closely related to 54-054-F, John
Alden Mason, South America, Colombia, Goajiro Indians,
1923.

54-053-F. William Lipkind, 1938.
    Brazil
       Caraja Indians
          Mato Grasso
             Animal imitations[?]; Laments; Unknown subjects
       Cayapo Indians
          Mato Grasso
             Unknown subjects
       Unknown culture groups
          Unknown locations
             Art songs, French

Number of cylinders: 178
Number of strips: 329
Sound quality of strips: G 11,   F 237,   P 71,   VP 5,
          U 5.
Degree of restriction: 1

   This is apparently a complete collection.
   Inconsistent linguistic symbols have made the
documentation of this collection difficult. The
collector's markings varied from one recording date to
another; this resulted in a quandary over which symbols to
use consistently for catalogue documentation.
   The singing style for these Brazilian songs is worthy of
note. Where the performance code indicates a duet, of two
men singing, it should be mentioned that two styles can be
included within this designation. For one, the singing is
in alternation: one man sings a "verse" line, and the
second man sings a repeated or "chorus" line. For
another, both men sing together, with many shouts included
in the song. Both of these duet styles are used
interchangeably throughout the Lipkind collection.
   The Lipkind cylinders have suffered generally from
tracking problems, varying speed and distortion.

54-054-F. John Alden Mason, 1923.
   Colombia
      Goajiro Indians
         La Calita (Chivita?)
            Dance songs
         La Guajira, Dibulla
            Dance songs; Festival songs; Flute music; Love
            songs; Street songs; Unknown subjects; War songs

Number of cylinders: 19
Number of strips: 69
Sound quality of strips: EX 2, G 37, F 30.
Degree of restriction: 2

   This collection is closely related to 54-052-F. The two
collections are separated according to Indian groups,
Arhuaco and Goajiro. The Goajiro cylinders also appear to
form a complete collection.
   The documentation for these South American cylinders is
fairly complete, and is augmented considerably by the
spoken announcements, presumably by Mason, at the
beginning of each recording. The announcements mention
the title of the composition, the name of the performer,
the location of the performance, and the date.
   The song descriptions are often general, as for example,
"Goajiro Indian song," or "Goajiro Indian duet."

54-055-F. Charles Wagley, ca. 1935.
   Brazil
      Caraja Indians
         Mato Grosso
            Unknown subjects
      Tapirapé Indians
         Mato Grosso
            Unknown subjects

Number of cylinders: 49
Number of strips: 50
Sound quality of strips: F 28, P 17, VP 5.
Degree of restriction: 1

   It is unfortunate that this South American field
collection is in such poor physical condition, since early
recordings from this part of the world are few and Charles
Wagley is a renowned anthropologist. By the time the
Cylinder Project staff undertook the task of cleaning and
recording the Wagley cylinders, nearly fifty years after
their original cutting, they had deteriorated terribly. A
heavy layer of mold covered each cylinder, making the
grooves almost indistinguishable. The result, in terms of
sound quality, was almost no volume for the recorded
voice, and very loud surface noise.
   The documentation for this collection, also
insufficient, has been acquired from hours of scrutiny of
faded inscriptions on the original cylinder boxes.

54-065-F. Natalie Curtis Burlin, 1915-1918.
   United States
      Africans[?]
         Virginia, Hampton
            Laments; Unknown subjects
      Unknown culture groups
         Virginia, Hampton
            Dance songs; Rain songs; Spirit songs; Unknown
            subjects
      Vandau (Bantu people)
         Virginia, Hampton
            Dance songs; Rain songs; Spirit songs; Unknown
            subjects
      Zulus
         Virginia, Hampton
            Dance songs; Laments; Love songs; Slave songs;
            Unknown subjects

Number of cylinders: 16
Number of strips: 20
Sound quality of strips: G 3, F 14, P 2, B 1.
Degree of restriction: 2

   The documentation for this incomplete collection has
been gathered from notes on the original cylinder boxes.
The researcher is also referred to: Natalie Curtis Burlin,
Songs and Tales from the Dark Continent. New York: G.
Schirmer, 1920.
   Two of the informants, Columbus Kamba Simango and
Madikane Cole, were students at the Hampton Institute,
where Mrs. Burlin also collected Afro-American spirituals.
(See related collection: 54-145-F.) These recordings
include rain songs, love songs, prayer songs, and a
demon's farewell songs.

54-076-F. Berthold Laufer, 1908.
   India
      Bengalis
         Sikkim, Darjeeling
            Theater music; Unknown subjects
      Hindus
         Sikkim, Darjeeling
            Love songs; Theater music
      Nepalese
         Sikkim, Darjeeling
            Flute music; Marriage rites and ceremonies
      Tibetans
         Sikkim, Darjeeling
            Drinking songs; Love songs; Unknown subjects
   India or Nepal or China
      Bengalis
         Unknown locations
            Flute music
      Hindus
         Unknown locations

                    Unknown subjects
            Tibetans
              Unknown locations
                Ballads; Unknown subjects; Women's songs

Number of cylinders: 26
Number of strips: 35
Sound quality of strips: G 4, F 25, P 4, B 2.
Degree of restriction: 2

    This collection of field recordings was received from
the Field Museum of Natural History in Chicago. At that
time, five of the cylinders were broken and two were
reported as missing. The 1983-84 Cylinder Project staff
was able to repair four of the five broken cylinders; the
two missing cylinders were also found and reunited with
the collection.
    The documentation for this collection is fairly
complete, including title or song genre, location of
recording, name of performer, and date of recording.
Informants are not always named specifically; for example,
one is listed as "Tibetan wandering singer." Genres are
also general, as with "Tibetan songs," or "love songs," or
"songs accompanied by fiddle." Some flute solos and duets
are included in the collection.

54-077-F. Gerhardt Kurt Laves, 1930.
    Australia
        Karadjeri (Australian people)
            West Australia, La Grange
                Dialogues; Funeral rites and ceremonies; Song
                cycles; Speeches, addresses, etc.; Stories,
                narratives and anecdotes (songs from)

Number of cylinders: 11
Number of strips: 21
Sound quality of strips: F 9, P 10, VP 2.
Degree of restriction: 1

    This is a small collection of cylinders, and it may not
be complete. Cylinder box documentation provides the bulk
of the information about these recordings, although the
announcements on the cylinders give some contextual data
and list text numbers for various songs.

54-078-F. George Amos Dorsey and/or Erich M. von
            Hornbostel, 1906[?].
    United States
        Igorot
            Illinois, Chicago[?]
                Unknown subjects

Number of cylinders: 2
Number of strips: 4

Sound quality of strips: G 3, F 1.
Degree of restriction: 2

   These two cylinders are strays from master boxes
originally belonging to a Dorsey Pawnee collection, 54-
011-F. Notes from the George Herzog catalogue give a clue
as to their origin: "Possibly recorded by Hornbostel in
the FM [Field Museum] in 1906 when he visited in US and
made recordings with Dorsey on the Pawnee Indian
Reservations."

54-079-F. Fay-Cooper Cole, 1907-1908.
   Philippines
      Bagobo (Philippine people)
         Dato-Ianykala [?]
            Unknown subjects
         Unknown locations
            Flute music[?]; Unknown subjects
      Batak (Palawan people)
         Mindusa [?]
            Healing songs
         Unknown locations
            Songs of thanks; Women's songs
      Bilaan (Philippine people)
         Santa Cruz
            Unknown subjects
         Unknown locations
            Unknown subjects
      Bukidnon (Philippine people)
         Central Mindanao, Dogondalahon
            Unknown subjects
         Dogondalahan
            Unknown subjects
         Langawan
            Unknown subjects
         Unknown locations
            Unknown subjects
      Isneg
         Tauit
            Unknown subjects
         Unknown locations
            Unknown subjects
      Kalagan (Philippine people)
         Unknown locations
            Unknown subjects
      Kalingas or Kalagan (Philippine people)
         Unknown locations
            Unknown subjects
      Mahampo (Philippine people) [?]
         Unknown locations
            Women's songs
      Mandaya (Philippine people)
         Unknown locations
            Funeral rites and ceremonies
      Mangyans (Philippine people)

        Unknown locations
          Unknown subjects
      Tagbanuas
        Dato
          Unknown subjects
        Unknown locations
          Festival songs; Instrumental music; Love songs;
          Unknown subjects
      Tinguianes
        Abra
          Rites and ceremonies; Songs for the dead
        Amtuagan
          Unknown subjects
        Balbalasang
          Unknown subjects
        Baok
          Unknown subjects
        Candon
          Unknown subjects
        Danok
          Drinking songs
        Gayaman
          Love songs
        Lagangilang
          Rites and ceremonies; Shamans' songs; Spirit
          songs; Unknown subjects
        Lakub
          Unknown subjects
        Langiden
          Unknown subjects
        Likuan Abra
          Unknown subjects
        Likuan
          Dance songs; Unknown subjects
        Manabo
          Dance songs; Drinking songs; Rites and
          ceremonies; Songs for the dead; Women's songs;
          Work songs; Unknown subjects
        Mayabo
          Unknown subjects
        Pancim [?]
          Unknown subjects
        Patok
          Dance songs; Drinking songs; Rites and
          ceremonies; Unknown subjects
        Santa Cruz [Island?]
          Unknown subjects
        Unknown locations
          Dance songs; Drinking songs; Rain songs; Rites
          and ceremonies; Spirit songs; Unknown subjects;
          Women's songs
      Unknown culture groups
        Batok
          Unknown subjects
        Sitay [?]
          Unknown subjects

        Unknown locations
            Flute music[?]; Healing songs; Music, Popular;
            Unknown subjects

Number of cylinders: 137
Number of strips: 145
Sound quality of strips: EX 1,   G 12,   F 50,   P 68,
        VP 10, B 4.
Degree of restriction: 2

   This large collection appears to be complete. The
documentation of the collection was improved by consulting
Fay-Cooper Cole. "The Tinguian," Field Museum of Natural
History, Anthropological Series 209, Vol. 14, No. 2.
Notes and transcriptions of Cole cylinder recordings by
Albert Gale are provided in Chapter 12 of this study.
Page numbers listed in the documentation of this
collection refer to "The Tinguian"; often specific music
transcriptions are designated.
   Informants for these cylinder recordings are listed by
first names only, as in Abra or Manabo.

54-080-F. Murray Barnson Emeneau, 1938.
   India
      Kota (Indic people)
         Unknown locations
            Instrumental music; Personal songs; Unknown
            subjects; Women's dance music
      Todas
         Unknown locations
            Dance songs; Funeral rites and ceremonies;
            Instrumental music; Laments; Morning songs;
            Nature songs; Unknown subjects
      Unknown culture groups
         Unknown locations
            Unknown subjects

Number of cylinders: 80
Number of strips: 141
Sound quality of strips: G 4,   F 84,   P 44,   VP 9.
Degree of restriction: 3

   Although the numbers for this collection are
consecutive, they were designated by George Herzog and not
Murray Emeneau; this leaves some doubt as to whether or
not the collection is complete.
   The documentation of the collection has resulted in even
greater uncertainties. The inscriptions on the cylinder
boxes, faded and enigmatic, were difficult to decipher.
They contain transliterations of Asian dialects, and they
make special use of some Greek alphabet characters and
some phonetic symbols.
   Three previously unidentified cylinders were found to be
test cylinders from the Emeneau collection. One of these
contains pronunciation samples and an announcement about

the people of rural India.

54-092-F. Carl Lumholtz, 1898.
    Mexico
        Tarahumare Indians
            Unknown locations
                Shamans' songs; Unknown subjects

Number of cylinders: 11
Number of strips: 25
Sound quality of strips: F 20, P 4, B 1.
Degree of restriction: 2

    This is a small but complete collection. Carl Lumholtz
made these recordings on the same expedition which
produced the Huichol Indian recordings: (see 54-093-F).
The documentation for the Tarahumare cylinders is not as
good as that for the Huichol. The original Tarahumare
boxes are only marked "Tarah. - C. Lumholtz-1898." The
researcher is referred to the following publication: Carl
Lumholtz. Unknown Mexico; A Record of Five Year's
Exploration Among the Tribes of the Western Sierra Madre;
In the Tierra Caliente of Tepic and Jalisco; and Among the
Tarascos of Michoacan. New York: Charles Scribner's Sons,
1902. Unknown Mexico contains transcriptions of some of
the Lumholtz cylinders.
    None of the cylinders is identified as being anything
more specific than a song. Only the last recording
contains the following remark in Dr. George Herzog's
worknotes: "C. Lumholtz singing German song and/or
shamanistic stuff?"

54-093-F. Carl Lumholtz, 1898.
    Mexico
        Huichol Indians
            Unknown locations
                Dance music[?]; Flute music; Instrumental music;
                Sones; Unknown subjects

Number of cylinders: 31
Number of strips: 62
Sound quality of strips: G 35, F 15, P 9, VP 3.
Degree of restriction: 2

    This is an early collection, apparently incomplete. A
related collection, 54-092-F, contains the Tarahumare
cylinders collected by Lumholtz on this field trip.
    Lumholtz, a Norwegian explorer, made four expeditions
into remote areas of Mexico in order to collect cultural
data for the American Museum of Natural History.
    Not all of the cylinders are clearly identified. Many
of the titles are in Spanish, as with "tamales de maíz
crudo," and "canción para llamar agua." There are a
few instumental compositions performed on the guitar and

the fiddle.

54-094-C. Joseph Kossuth Dixon, 1909.
   United States
      Siksika Indians
         Montana, Crow Agency
            Hunting songs; Love songs; Scalp dance songs;
            Unknown subjects; War songs

Number of cylinders: 27
Number of strips: 27
Sound quality of strips: EX 19,   U 8.
Degree of restriction: 2

   This is a collection of Edison commercial reproductions
of the field recordings Dixon made on the Wanamaker
Historical Expedition (2nd: 1909). The detailed
announcements on the cylinder recordings give information
about the name of the song, the name of the singer, the
identification of the research expedition, the culture
group of the singer, the date, and the location of the
recording.
   There are five separate recordings among these nineteen
cylinders; the rest are copies of those five recordings.
The genres represented are war songs, love songs, and
hunting songs. Photographs of some of the informants for
this collection may be found at the I.U. William Hammond
Mathers Musem.

Related collections: 54-102-C, 54-108-C, and 54-109-C.

54-095-F. George Bird Grinnell, 1897.
   United States
      British Americans
         Unknown locations
            Unknown subjects
      Siksika Indians
         Montana, Kalispell
            Society songs
         Montana, Piegan Agency
            Dance songs; Duck dance songs; Hunting songs;
            Lodge songs; Love songs; Medicine songs; Scalp
            dance songs; Society songs; Unknown subjects; War
            songs; Weasel dance songs; Wolf dance songs

Number of cylinders: 25
Number of strips: 58
Sound quality of strips: F 40,   P 7,   VP 6,   B 4,   U 1.
Degree of restriction: 2

   George Bird Grinnell is best known for his work as an
American naturalist; in 1886 he founded the first chapter
of what later became the National Audubon Society. His
first trip to the West, collecting fossils for the Peabody

Museum of Yale University, brought him in contact with various North American Indians. For the next forty years, he studied Indian culture every summer.

The documentation for this collection was compiled from inscriptions on the cylinder boxes and information from the American Museum of Natural History Phonograph Recordings Catalogue, where the genres, dates, and informants' names are clearly indicated. This collection includes four previously unidentified test cylinders which feature Grinnell and "J.J.W" singing English, Italian, and French songs.

Grinnell's informants were Mary Evans, James White Calf, Black-Looks, Chews-Black-Bones, Rides-at-the-Door, Wipes-His-Eyes, Cross-Guns, and George Starr.

A related collection is 54-104-F (Arapaho, Cheyenne, and Omaha), recorded on the same expedition.

54-096-F. Clark Wissler, 1903-04.
    Canada
      Kainah Indians (item)
        Alberta, Blood Reservation
          Medicine bundle songs; Moon songs; Tobacco dance
          songs; Unknown subjects
    United States
      Piegan Indians
        Montana, Blackfoot Reservation
          Grass dance songs; Medicine songs; Pipe songs;
          Prayers
      Piegan Indians (item)
        Montana, Blackfoot Reservation
          Bird dance songs; Bull dance songs; Courting
          dance songs; Deer dance songs; Game songs; Grass
          dance songs; Lodge songs; Medicine bundle songs;
          Medicine songs; Pipe songs; Prayers; Rites and
          ceremonies; Robe ceremonies; Scalp dance songs;
          Society songs; Stick game songs; Sun dance songs;
          Tea dance songs; Unknown subjects; War songs;
          Wolf dance songs; Women's songs
    [United States?]
      Siksika Indians (item)
        [Montana, Blackfoot Reservation ?]
          Prayers; Stories, narratives and anecdotes;
          Unknown subjects
    United States or Canada
      Siksika Indians
        Unknown locations
          Unknown subjects
      Unknown culture groups
        Unknown locations
          Unknown subjects

Number of cylinders: 148
Number of strips: 290
Sound quality of strips: EX 6, G 175, F 83, P 17,
        VP 2, B 6, U 1.

Degree of restriction: 2

Clark Wissler recorded this collection on an expedition
sponsored by the American Museum of Natural History. The
AMNH Catalog of Phonograph Recordings indicates cylinders
which relate to artifacts Wissler collected for the
Museum. This catalog was the primary source of
documentation. Inscriptions on the cylinder boxes and
Wissler's notes found inside the cylinder boxes were also
useful.
For the most part, Wissler did not record his
informants' names, but did identify Bear Child and Bull
Child.

54-097-F. Roland Burrage Dixon and D. S. Spencer, 1910.
   United States
      Maidu Indians
         California, Genessee
            Unknown subjects
         California, Moorestown
            Dance songs; Game songs
         Unknown locations
            Unknown subjects
      [Maidu?] Indians
         Unknown locations
            Basket songs; Dance songs; Gambling songs; War
            songs; Women's songs

Number of cylinders: 21
Number of strips: 65
Sound quality of strips: G 32, F 23, P 8, VP 2.
Degree of restriction: 2

This collection was recorded for the American Museum of
Natural History. The performers, Bill Brooks from
Moorestown, and Ti Young and K. Reeves from Genessee, sing
a wide variety of songs from the Maidu tradition. Notes
on slips found inside the cylinder boxes offer information
about how and when the songs were to performed, and some
song texts and translations.

54-098-F. Samuel Alfred Barrett, and Alfred Louis and
           Henrietta Kroeber, 1905-08.
   United States
      Klamath Indians
         Oregon, Klamath Reservation
            Gambling songs; Game songs; Unknown subjects
      Mohave Indians
         California
            Rites and ceremonies
      Pomo Indians
         California, San Francisco
            Dance songs
      Yukian Indians

California, Round Valley Reservation
    Deer songs; Doctors' songs; Feather dance songs;
    Hunting songs; Men's dance songs; Rites and
    ceremonies; Women's dance songs
Yurok Indians
    California
    Brush dance songs; Dance songs

Number of cylinders: 12
Number of strips: 12
Sound quality of strips: F 1, P 5, VP 6.
Degree of restriction: 2

   This is a small collection, most likely incomplete, as
the collector's numbers are not in consecutive order. The
textual information for the collection has come from the
American Museum of Natural History Phonorecordings
Catalogue, and the dates of the recordings have been found
on the original cylinder boxes. In most cases, these
cylinders have complete documentation. Some documentation
provides contextual data concerning the ceremonial dances:
details about the costumes, or specifications concerning
who should dance.

Reference:
Kroeber, Alfred L. Handbook of the Indians of California.
Bureau of American Ethnology, Bulletin 78, 1925.

54-099-F. Unknown collector, no date.
    United States
    Indians of North America (unidentified)
        Unknown locations
        Scalp dance songs[?]; Unknown subjects

Number of cylinders: 3
Number of strips: 3
Sound quality of strips: EX 1, G 1, F 1.
Degree of restriction: 2

   The documentation for these cylinders has come from
notes on the original cylinder boxes. The notes are full
of question marks, and the information is brief. The
informant is possibly a man, Dave Heruska, for the first
two cylinders; there is no information for the third. The
written notes are marked Omaha ? Pawnee ?, for all three
recordings.

54-100-F. Collector unknown, no date.
    [United States]
    Chippewa Indians
        Unknown locations
        Unknown subjects

        Unknown culture groups
          Unknown locations
            Unknown subjects

Number of cylinders: 43
Number of strips: 114
Sound quality of strips: F 59, P 22, VP 19, B 14.
Degree of restriction: 2

    There is very little documentation for these cylinders.
A few of them have the word "Ojibwa" etched on the edges;
some of the recordings, according to the Cylinder Project
technicians, sound like European melodies. This adds
further confusion to the understanding of the collection.
    Some of the performances are of a male group of singers,
some are male solos, and some are female solo songs.
Several of the group songs include a drum accompaniment.

54-101-F. George Herzog and Leslie A. White, 1927.
    United States
      Acoma Indians
        New Mexico, Acomita
          Buffalo dance songs; Festival songs; Hunting
          songs; Rites and ceremonies
      Acoma Indians (inf.); Comanche Indians (item)
        New Mexico, Acomita
          Dance songs
      Acoma Indians (inf.); Mescalero Indians (item)
        New Mexico, Acomita
          Dance songs
      Acoma Indians (inf.); Mexicans (item)
        New Mexico, Acomita
          Hymns
      Acoma Indians (inf.); Navaho Indians (items)
        New Mexico, Acomita
          Dance songs; Kachinas

Number of cylinders: 15
Number of strips: 18
Sound quality of strips: G 10, F 8.
Degree of restriction: 2

    George Herzog's music transcriptions and field notes
have provided valuable documentation for this incomplete
collection. Although Leslie White and George Herzog
collaborated in making these recordings, the collection
was divided between them. White's 1927 Acoma recordings
may be found in collection 60-004-F. The single informant
is identified only as James.

54-102-C. Joseph Kossuth Dixon, 1909.
    United States
      Apache Indians
        Montana, Crow Agency
          Dance songs; Hunting songs

Number of cylinders: 12
Number of strips: 12
Sound quality of strips: EX 6,   G 5,   NR 1.
Degree of restriction: 1

   These Edison commercial recordings contain five copies
of the collector's cylinder number one and six copies of
number two. The documentation is taken from Dixon's
announcements at the beginning of each cylinder. These
announcements are unusually complete, containing the name
of the songs, the name of the singer, the identification
of the research expedition, the culture group of the
singer, the date, and the location of the recordings.
   The original field recordings, not held by the Archives
of Traditional Music, were made for the Wanamaker
Historical Expedition (2nd: 1909).
   Photographs of some of the informants for this
collection may be found at the I.U. William Hammond
Mathers Museum.

Related collections: 54-094, 54-108, and 54-109-C.

54-103-F. Pliny Earle Goddard, 1909-1910; 1914.
    United States
      Apache Indians
        Arizona
          Rites and ceremonies
        Arizona, San Carlos Indian Reservation
          Dance songs; Deer dance songs; Hunting songs;
          Puberty rites, (female); Stories, narratives and
          anecdotes; Unknown subjects
      Jicarilla Indians
        New Mexico, Jicarilla Indian Reservation
          Dance songs; War dance songs
      Mescalero Indians
        Arizona, San Carlos Indian Reservation
          Unknown subjects
        Arizona, White Mountain Apache Reservation
          Stories, narratives and anecdotes, (songs
          from)[?]; Unknown subjects
        New Mexico, Mescalero Apache Reservation
          Rites and ceremonies
        Unknown locations
          Flute music; Rites and ceremonies; Unknown
          subjects

Number of cylinders: 157
Number of strips: 172
Sound quality of strips: G 1,   F 44,   P 67,   VP 58,   B 1,

          U 1.
Degree of restriction: 2

   This is a large collection, containing cylinder
recordings from various Goddard field trips. It is hard
to determine whether any of these scattered groups
constitute complete collections, as the original
collector's numbers are inconsistent.
   Many of these cylinders are representative of the songs
performed for a lengthy ceremony, ganhi, in which men
dance around a fire and dress themselves to represent the
gods of the mountains.
   Other recordings are from a larger Mescalero Apache
ceremony, gotal, which involves the erection of a sacred
lodge and the performance of a series of songs in honor of
the sun.

References:
Goddard, Pliny Earle. Indians of the Southwest. New
York: American Museum of Natural History, 1931.

_____. Myths and Tales from the San Carlos
Apache, in Anthropological Papers, Vol. 24, Pt. I. New
York: American Museum of Natural History, 1918.

_____. White Mountain Apache Myths and
Tales, in Anthropological Papers, Vol. 24, Pt. II. New
York: American Museum of Natural History, 1919.

_____. Jicarilla Apache Texts, in
Anthropological Papers, Vol. 8. New York: American
Museum of Natural History, 1911.

_____. "Gotal--A Mescalero Apache
Ceremony." Anthropological Essays: Putnam Anniversary
Volume. New York: Stechert and Co., 1909, pp. 385-394.

54-104-F. George Bird Grinnell, 1897-1898.
    United States
      Cheyenne Indians
        Montana, Lame Deer
          Bear songs; Camp songs; Chiefs' songs; Courting
          dance songs; Dance songs[?]; Doctors' songs;
          Gambling songs; Ghost dance songs; Ghost songs;
          Girls' dance songs; Hand game songs; Healing
          songs[?]; Horse songs; Lodge songs; Love songs;
          Medicine songs; Prayer songs; Rites and
          ceremonies[?]; Sacred songs[?]; Social dance
          songs; Society songs; Victory songs; Wolf songs
      Cheyenne Indians (inf.)
        Montana, Lame Deer
          Dance songs; Fox dance songs[?]; Unknown subjects
      Unknown culture groups
        Unknown locations
          Love songs

Number of cylinders: 23
Number of strips: 71
Sound quality of strips: G 3, F 30, P 24, VP 10, B 4.
Degree of restriction: 2

   Documentation for this collection is good; written
inscriptions on the original cylinder boxes supplement
spoken announcements on the recordings themselves. A
number of informants perform the songs, sometimes
separately, and sometimes as a group. In each case, the
singers are listed by an English translation of the Indian
name, as with Little Head, Dives Backwards, and Wild Hog.
However, there are significant problems in matching the
information to the proper cylinder. The collector's
numbers are not consecutive and through the years some
cylinders were placed in the wrong boxes.

Related collection: 54-095-F.

54-105-F. William Jones, 1903-1905.
   United States
      Chippewa Indians
         Minnesota, Leech Lake Indian Reservation
            Chants; Drinking songs; Feather dance songs;
            Lodge songs; Love songs; Moccasin dance songs;
            Moccasin game songs; Night dance songs; Scalp
            dance songs; Unknown subjects; Women's dance
            songs

Number of cylinders: 55
Number of strips: 95
Sound quality of strips: G 52, F 36, P 7.
Degree of restriction: 2

   Most of these cylinders contain recordings of Midewiwin
songs and chants. No singers are named.

Reference:
Jones, William. Ojibway Texts, in American Ethnological
Society Publications, Vol. 7, Pt. 1, Franz Boas, ed.
Leyden: 1917.

   The above volume documents the work done by William
Jones when he was employed as a research assistant for the
Carnegie Institution and charged with the study of the
Ojibwa tribes. Most of his investigations were carried
out north of Lake Superior. He later accepted a position
with the Field Museum of Natural History of Chicago. He
took the manuscript, Ojibwa Texts, with him to his next
assignment, the Philippine Islands, with the intention of
working on it during his free time. During his research,
he was captured and killed by native islanders. After
many years Jones' manuscript was recovered by a staff
member of the Field Museum and published.

54-106-F. George Herzog, 1927.
   United States
     Cochiti Indians
      New Mexico, Santa Fe
        Antelope dance songs; Bird dance songs; Buffalo
        dance songs; Corn dance songs; Dance songs; Deer
        dance songs; Eagle dance songs; Hunting dance
        songs; Reindeer dance songs; Rites and
        ceremonies; Spring songs; War dance songs
     Cochiti Indians (inf.); Comanche Indians (item)
      New Mexico, Santa Fe
        Unknown subjects

Number of cylinders: 22
Number of strips: 28
Sound quality of strips: G 2, F 12, P 13, VP 1.
Degree of restriction: 2

   The performers for this collection are Ruys Suina, an 18
year old boy, and Epiphano Pecos, a 27 year old man.
Most of the songs are dance songs. In some cases, the
documentation indicates that the song is the singer's own
composition. The documentation includes George Herzog's
field notes and transcriptions of the music and texts for
seventeen of the cylinders. Five transcriptions were
published in Herzog's "A Comparison of Pueblo and Pima
Musical Styles," Journal of American Folk-Lore, Vol. 49
(1936) pp. 283-417.

54-107-F. Frank Gouldsmith Speck, ca. 1905.
   United States
     Creek Indians
      Oklahoma, Taskigi [Tuskegee?]
        Buffalo dance songs; Dance songs; Duck dance
        songs; Feather dance songs; Fish dance songs;
        Game songs; Horse dance songs; Hunting songs;
        Medicine songs; Owl dance songs; Rabbit dance
        songs; Stories, narratives and anecdotes; Unknown
        subjects; War dance songs
      Oklahoma, Tulsa
        Feather dance songs
   [United States]
     Shawnee Indians
      [Oklahoma?]
        Love songs
     Unknown culture groups
      [Oklahoma?]
        Unknown subjects

Number of cylinders: 50
Number of strips: 55
Sound quality of strips: G 4, F 38, P 13.
Degree of restriction: 2

   This group of cylinders, along with collection 54-141-F,

form a complete collection. Speck's publication,
<u>Ceremonial Songs of the Creek and Yuchi Indians</u>,
University of Pennsylvania, Anthropolical Publications,
Vol. 1, No. 2, Philadelphia, 1911, was used to provide
documentation for both collections. This volume contains
numerous music transcriptions made by Jacob D. Sapir.
   A key informant is Kabitcimala (Leslie Cloud).

Reference:
Cassell, Nancy A. "American Ethnologist Frank Gouldsmith
Speck," <u>Resound</u>, Vol. II, No. 1 (Jan., 1983), pp. 3-4.

54-108-C. Joseph Kossuth Dixon, 1909.
    United States
       Crow Indians
          Montana, Crow Agency
             Dance songs; Feast songs; Lodge songs; Owl dance
             songs; Songs of thanks; Tobacco dance songs;
             Unknown subjects; Victory songs; War dance songs;
             War songs

Number of cylinders: 96
Number of strips: 96
Sound quality of strips: EX 6, G 22, F 35, P 15,
          VP 1, U 2, NR 15.
Degree of restriction: 2

   These cylinders are Edison commercial reproductions of
Joseph Dixon's field recordings for the Wanamaker
Historical Expedition (2nd: 1909). There are seventeen
separate selections in the collection, and the rest of the
cylinders are duplicate copies. Each cylinder has an
extensive narrative announcement which states the name of
the song, the name of the singer, the identification of
the research expedition, the culture group of the singer,
the date, and the location of the recording.
   Photographs of some of the informants for this
collection may be found at the I.U. William Hammond
Mathers Museum.

Related collections: 54-094-C, 54-102-C, and 54-109-C.

54-109-C. Joseph Kossuth Dixon, 1909.
    United States
       Dakota Indians
          Montana, Crow Agency
             Chiefs' songs; Love songs; Speeches, addresses,
             etc.; Unknown subjects; War songs

Number of cylinders: 35
Number of strips: 35
Sound quality of strips: EX 4, G 2, B 1, NR 28.
Degree of restriction: 2

   These thirty-five cylinders are mass produced Edison
Bacolite copies of Joseph Dixon's original field
cylinders, recorded for the Wanamaker Expedition (2nd:
1909). Six of the cylinders are separate selections, and
the others are copies of those selections.
   The documentation comes entirely from Dixon's
announcements at the beginning of each cylinder recording.
Each cylinder has an extensive introduction which states
the name of the song, the name of the singer, the
identification of the research expedition, the culture
group of the singer, the date, and location of the
recording.
   Photographs of some of the informants for this
collection may be found at the I.U. William Hammond
Mathers Museum.

Related collections: Dixon, 54-094-C, 54-102-C, 54-108-C.

54-110-F. George Herzog, 1928.
    United States
      Dakota Indians
        North Dakota, Standing Rock Reservation
          Bear songs; Begging songs; Buffalo dance songs;
          Buffalo songs; Children's game songs; Coyote
          songs; Dance songs; Dream songs; Drinking songs;
          Feast songs; Ghost dance songs; Grass dance
          songs; Hiding dance songs; Hiding game songs;
          Horse dance songs; Love songs; Medicine dance
          songs; Medicine songs; Night dance songs; Peyote
          songs; Prayers; Rabbit dance songs; Rites and
          ceremonies; Society songs; Songs of honor and
          praise; Sun dance songs; Unknown subjects;
          Victory songs; Vision songs
      Dakota Indians (inf.); Crow Indians (item)
        North Dakota, Standing Rock Reservation
          Dance songs
      Dakota Indians (inf.); Arikara Indians (item)
        North Dakota, Standing Rock Reservation
          Dance songs; Snake dance songs

Number of cylinders: 195
Number of strips: 210
Sound quality of strips: G 3, F 160, P 15, VP 2.
Degree of restriction: 2

   This is a complete collection of cylinders recorded on
an American Museum of Natural History expedition to Fort
Yates, in the Standing Rock Reservation. The names of the
informants are listed, sometimes by dialect names, as with
Watc'i'bidiza, and sometimes by translated names, as with
Edward Afraid of Hawk. Occasionally the manner of
composition is noted, as, for example, two songs of the
tokana (fox) society, "given to a boy in a vision."
   Documentation for this collection includes George
Herzog's field notebooks, music transcriptions, and text

translations for many of the songs recorded.

References:
Herzog, George. "Special Song Types in North American
Indian Music." Zeitschrift für Musikwissenschaft
3:1/2, pp. 1-11, 1935. (SCY 3244; 3391; 3395)

Herzog, George. "Plains Ghost Dance and Great Basin
Music." American Anthropologist 37:3, pp. 403-419, 1935.
(SCY 3337, Collector's no. 93.)

54-112-F.   James John Walker, 1908.
     United States
       Dakota Indians
         South Dakota, Pine Ridge
           Bear songs; Buffalo songs; Dance songs; Festival
           songs; Horse dance songs; Horse songs; Lightning
           songs[?]; Medicine songs; Scalp dance songs;
           Scalp songs; Scouts' songs; Sun dance songs;
           Unknown subjects; Victory songs
       Dakota Indians (inf.); Omaha Indians (item)
         South Dakota, Pine Ridge
           Dance songs
       Dakota Indians (inf.); Oglala Indians (item)
         South Dakota, Pine Ridge
           Love songs; Puberty rites (female); Unknown
           subjects

Number of cylinders: 64
Number of strips: 66
Sound quality of strips: G 3,   F 38,   P 20,   VP 2,   B 3.
Degree of restriction: 2

   This collection is a combination of recordings deposited
in the American Museum of Natural History in 1908 and in
1909. It is incomplete.
There are some gaps in the documentation for the Walker
cylinders. Informants are not consistently mentioned;
neither are the dates of the performances. Some of the
songs, however, do contain some contextual information, as
with an Oglala Indian song, "sung when starting on a long
journey," or a dedication song, "sung when making medicine
and other mysterious things." There are occasional group
songs, accompanied by bells, rattles and membranophones.

54-113-F.   Constance Goddard Dubois, 1905.
     United States
       Diegueño Indians
         California
           Dance songs; Festival songs; Flute music; Funeral
           rites and ceremonies; Gambling songs;
           Instrumental music; Puberty rites (female);
           Unknown subjects
         California, San Jose, Warner's Ranch

        Dance songs

Number of cylinders: 15
Number of strips: 46
Sound quality of strips: G 13, F 23, P 10.
Degree of restriction: 2

    This is a small incomplete collection recorded by Dubois
for the Ethnological and Archeological Survey of
California, conducted by the University of California,
Berkeley. Her recordings of the Luiseño Indians of
California may be found under accession number 54-123-F.
    Most of the documentation for these cylinders was drawn
from inscriptions on the cylinder boxes.

54-114-F. George Herzog, 1927.
    United States
      Diegueño Indians
        California, Campo
          Bird dance songs; Dance songs; Game songs;
          Laments; Puberty rites, (female); Rites and
          ceremonies
      Diegueño Indians (inf.); Yuma Indians (item)
        California, Campo
          Dance songs; Wildcat dance songs

Number of cylinders: 17
Number of strips: 30
Sound quality of strips: G 27, F 3.
Degree of restriction: 2

    This small but complete collection was recorded for the
American Museum of Natural History. The documentation is
supplemented by George Herzog's field notes and text
transcriptions.
    There is one informant for all of the recordings, Mrs.
Kate Coleman, "about 45 years old," who said that she had
learned some of her songs from the Yuma Indians but did
not know their meaning (SCY 3552-3561). Herzog noted that
many of the songts were usually accompanied by a rattle--
either a gourd or a spice box.

Reference:
Herzog, George. "The Yuman Musical Style," Journal of
American Folk-Lore, Vol. 41 (1928) pp. 183-231.

54-115-F. George Comer, 1903-1909.
    Canada
      Eskimos
        Northwest Territories
          Childrens' game songs; Deer songs; Hunting songs;
          Hymns; Rites and ceremonies; Speeches, addresses,
          etc.; Stories, narratives, and anecdotes; Unknown
          subjects

        Northwest Territories, District of Keewatin, Cape
        Fullerton
          Hunting songs
      Unknown culture groups
        Northwest Territories
          Hunting songs; Stories, narratives and anecdotes;
          Unknown subjects

Number of cylinders: 64
Number of strips: 65
Sound quality of strips: G 39,   F 23,   P 2,   VP 1.
Degree of restriction: 2

   This is a complete collection of cylinders, resulting
from a remarkable intereaction between George Comer, the
captain of a whaling ship, the Era, and the Eskimo groups
he encountered during his excursions into the northern
Hudson Bay regions. Before the whaling period, white
contacts with Eskimo culture had been few. His account of
the expedition takes the form of a diary: Ross, W.
Gillies, ed. An Artic Whaling Diary: The Journal of
Captain George Comer in Hudson Bay 1903-1905. Toronto:
University of Toronto Press, 1984. Many of the Eskimos
listed under "Natives" in the index of this diary are the
informants who recite and sing for the cylinder
recordings.
   A good number of the songs performed refer to hunting;
others have to do with ceremonies, such as name
exchanging, or shamanistic ritual songs. There are a few
narrative accounts of whaling adventures and previous
expeditions.
   All of the cylinders contain English announcements.
Most of them are exceptionally clear recordings
considering the conditions under which they were first
made.
   A small number of music transcriptions made by George
Herzog are a part of the documentation to this collection.

54-116-F. Crocker Land Expedition (1913-1917), 1917.
   Canada
     Eskimos
       Northwest Territories
         Unknown subjects

Number of cylinders: 12
Number of strips: 12
Sound quality of strips: F 6,   VP 4,   B 2.
Degree of restriction: 2

   These cylinders were first a group of ten; two
additional cylinders were identified and added to this
collection by the Cylinder Project Staff.
   The location of the recordings is the Arctic region of
Canada. The cylinders include unidentified songs,
attempts to record auks, and one of "men working dogs."

54-117-F.   Gilbert Livingstone Wilson, 1906-1909.
   United States
      Hidatsa Indians
         Unknown locations
            Love songs
      [Hidatsa Indians or Mandan Indians]
         Unknown locations
            Bear songs; Buffalo dance songs; Purification
            songs; Snake songs; Unknown subjects
      Mandan Indians
         Unknown locations
            Buffalo dance songs; Love songs; Prayers; War
            songs

Number of cylinders: 22
Number of strips: 22
Sound quality of strips: G 9,   F 10, P 3.
Degree of restriction: 2

   This small collection is very well documented. One of
the cylinders in the collection, a "Mandan Love Song," was
transcribed and published by George Herzog in Zeitschrift
für Vergleichende Musik Wissenshaft, Vol. 3, Nos. 1-2, pp.
1-11, 1935. The collection also received attention in
Weitzner, Bella, ed. "Notes on the Hidatsa Indians based
on Data Recorded by the late Gilbert L. Wilson."
Anthropological Papers of the American Museum of Natural
History, Vol. 56, Part 2, 1979.
   The informants are identified as Packs Wolf, Good Road,
Calf Woman, and Good Bird. The collection includes an
oddity, a recitation of the Lord's Prayer in Mandan,
possibly done by G.L. Wilson himself.

54-118-F. Natalie Curtis Burlin, 1903.
   United States
      British Americans
         Arizona, Canyon Diablo
            Unknown subjects
      Hopi Indians
         Arizona
            Flute songs; Grinding songs; Kachinas; Lullabies;
            Prayers; Rain songs; Unknown subjects
         Arizona, Canyon Diablo
            Kachinas; Love songs; Unknown subjects
         Arizona, Oraibi
            Basket songs; Boys' dance songs; Dance songs;
            Girls' dance songs; Grinding songs; Kachinas;
            Lullabies; Prayers; Rain songs; Unknown subjects;
            Women's songs
         Arizona, [Oraibi]
            Basket songs; Kachinas
      Hopi Indians[?] (inf.); Navaho Indians (item); Zuñi
      Indians (item)
         Arizona
         Kachinas

        Navaho Indians
          Arizona
            Sacred music; Unknown subjects
          Arizona, Canyon Diablo
            Dance songs; Grinding songs; War songs
          Arizona, Fields
            Greeting songs; Unknown subjects
          Arizona, [Fields]
            Unknown subjects
          Arizona, Oraibi
            Unknown subjects
        Unknown culture groups
          Unknown locations
            Unknown subjects
        Zuñi Indians
          Arizona, Oraibi
            Kachinas

Number of cylinders: 85
Number of strips: 85
Sound quality of strips: G 3, F 37, P 29, VP 10, B 5,
      U 1.
Degree of restriction: 2

   In his summary of Natalie Curtis Burlin, Allen Johnson
(Dictionary of American Biography, 1943) states that
after a thorough European classical music training,
Natalie Curtis Burlin returned to America where "it was
evidently her purpose to continue her career as a pianist,
but while visiting...in Arizona she became interested in
the Indians of that region and their music." It is to the
advantage of the discipline of ethnomusicology that such a
diversion took place. The documentation for these
cylinders is fairly complete; a fortunate circumstance due
to the present sound quality of the cylinders. The
informants are numerous and the types of song widely
varied. Solo and group performances are mainly without
the accompaniment of percussive instruments.

Related collection: 54-027 Burlin, Natalie Curtis, Hopi
Indians.

Reference:
The Indian's Book, New York: Dover Publications, 1968.

54-119-F. George Herzog, 1928.
    United States
      Hopi Indians
        New York
          Kachina songs

Number of cylinders: 1
Number of strips: 1
Sound quality of strips: F 1.
Degree of restriction: 2

   This cylinder is a recording of a kachina song sung by
four unidentified Hopi Indians at the American Museum of
Natural History.

54-120-F. George Herzog, 1927.
    United States
      Hupa Indians
        California, Hupa
          Brush dance songs; Dance songs; Doctors' songs;
          Flower dance songs; Gambling songs; Jumping dance
          songs; Kick dance songs; Love songs; Men's songs;
          Stick game songs; War dance songs; Women's songs

Number of cylinders: 22
Number of strips: 43
Sound quality of strips: G 38, F 5.
Degree of restriction: 2

   This is a complete collection of cylinders recorded for
the American Museum of Natural History. It has been
documented in an article by Helen H. Roberts, "The First
Salmon Ceremony of the Karok Indians," American
Anthropologist, Vol. 34, No. 3 (1932), pp. 426-440, which
contains transcriptions of two of Dr. Herzog's Karok
recordings. Eight separate informants provide the songs
for this collection. A few doctor's songs contain bits of
contextual data, as with "doctor song when sucking out the
pain."

54-121-F. Franz Boas [and John Comfort Fillmore?],
           [1893?].
    [United States?]
      Kwakiutl Indians
        [Illinois, Chicago?]
          Unknown subjects

Number of cylinders: 37
Number of strips: 50
Sound quality of strips: G 2, F 32, P 12, VP 3, B 1.
Degree of restriction: 2

   There are some curious contradictions in this
collection, especially concerning the location and the
date of the recordings. According to Cylinder Project
documentor Carol F. Inman, "Boas listed the collection in
the American Museum of Natural History Phonorecordings
Catalogue as recorded at Fort Rupert, Vancouver Island but
his preface to the 1895 U.S. National Museum report
stated, 'A series of phonographic records of songs
belonging to the ceremonials were transcribed by Mr. John
C. Fillmore and myself. I also had opportunity to verify

many of the phonographic records by letting the Indians
repeat the songs two years after the records had been
taken.' The latter statement would seem to indicate that
cylinders for the 1895 publication were recorded by Boas
and Fillmore at the World's Columbian Exposition, Chicago,
1893, where Boas was responsible for the organization of a
Kwakiutl village on the Midway Plaisance."
    The titles of the songs in this collection are phonetic
transliterations of the Kwakiutl language, written on the
original cylinder boxes, and noted in the American Museum
of Natural History Phonorecordings Calalogue. A few text
transcriptions made by Boas have been found among George
Herzog's papers, and are available as documentation.

References:
Boas, Franz. "The Social Organization and Secret Societies
of the Kwakiutl Indians." United States National Museum
Report, 1895.

_____. "Songs of the Kwakiutl," Internationale
Archiv für Ethnographie, Supplement to Vol. IX, pp.1-9.

Related collections: 54-035-F; 83-917-F.

54-122-F. George Herzog, 1927.
    United States
        Laguna Indians
            New Mexico, Laguna Pueblo
                Dance songs; Grinding songs; Kachinas; Medicine
                songs; Rain dance songs
        Laguna Indians (inf.); Comanche Indians (item)
            New Mexico, Laguna Pueblo
                Dance songs

Number of cylinders: 24
Number of strips: 27
Sound quality of strips: G 26, F 1.
Degree of restriction: 2

    The key informants in this collection cylinders are a
Mrs. Pina, also an informant of E.C. Parsons, and
Kayatyci, an 85 year old man from Messita, New Mexico.
The documentation for the collection has come from Dr.
Herzog's work notes, and his own text and music
transcriptions of all but seven of the cylinders.
  Mrs. Pina's songs are sung without accompaniment;
Kayatyci's songs frequently have a drum accompaniment.

Reference:
Herzog, George. "A Comparison of Pueblo and Pima Musical
Styles," Journal of American Folklore, Vol. 49. No. 194
(1936), pp. 283-417.

54-123-F.   Constance Goddard DuBois, 1906.
    United States
        Luiseño Indians
            California, San Diego County
                Coyote dance songs; Dance songs; Festival songs;
                Funeral rites and ceremonies; Instructional
                songs; Rites and ceremonies; Sacred songs;
                Unknown subjects; Wildcat dance songs; Women's
                songs
        Unknown culture groups
            California, San Diego County
                Unknown subjects

Number of cylinders: 30
Number of strips: 42
Sound quality of strips: G 33,   F 6,   P 2,   U 1.
Degree of restriction: 2

    This collection was recorded at various sites
surrounding the San Luiseño reservation. Constance
Dubois did her research among the Luiseño Indians for the
Ethnological and Archaeological Survey of California,
through a grant from Pearl A. Hearst.
    The performers are identified as Jose Luis Albanez,
Salvador Cuervas, Juan de Dios, Margarita Subish, Ha-ta-
kek, and Laguna Jim. A few of the melodies were published
in Dubois, Constance G. The Religion of the Luiseño
Indians of Southern California. University of California
Publications in American Archaeology and Ethnology, Vol.
8, No. 3, 1908. The melodies are referred to by cylinder
number.

Related collection: Dubois, Diegueño Indians (54-113-F).

54-124-F.   George Herzog, 1927.
    United States
        Mohave Indians
            Arizona, Needles
                Bird dance song
            Arizona, Yuma
                Dance songs; Rabbit dance songs; Unknown subjects

Number of cylinders: 31
Number of strips: 36
Sound quality of strips: G 26,   F 7,   P 3.
Degree of restriction: 2

    George Herzog's work notes for this collection indicate
that he made these recordings in Needles and Yuma,
Arizona. Current atlases indicate that Needles is in
California, just west of the Arizona border. The
collector's designation has been preserved in the
documentation.
    All of these recordings are of Mojave song series: the
Pleides song series, the Rabbit dance songs series, the

Vinyəmulye pá·tc , and the Tumánp Vanyúme series. There are
two informants, Sitcó'm·á·ì, a man of about 45 years, and
John Carter, a man of about 55 years. The songs are
accompanied either by the beating of a basket or by the
shaking of a gourd rattle. All but one of the recordings
made by Sitcó'm·á·ì conclude with the singer's precise
"ha ha".

George Herzog's field notes and transcriptions of the
music and song texts to all but five of the cylinders are
available as documentation. Fourteen of the
transcriptions were published in Dr. Herzog's article,
"The Yuman Musical Style," Journal of American Folk-Lore,
Vol. 41 (1921) pp. 183-231.

54-125-F. Washington Matthews, ca. 1893-1901.
    United States
        Navaho Indians
            Arizona and New Mexico
                Chants; Grinding songs; Lodge songs; Prayers;
                Pumpkin songs; Rites and ceremonies; Speeches,
                addresses, etc.; Thunder songs; Tobacco songs;
                Unknown subjects; War songs

Number of cylinders: 76
Number of strips: 77
Sound quality of strips: F 13, P 24, VP 39, U 1.
Degree of restriction: 2

Cylinder Project staff member Nancy A. Cassell has
prepared a concordance for this collection which combines
information received from Katherine Spencer Halpern at the
Wheelright Museum, Santa Fe, New Mexico, the American
Museum of Natural History Phonorecordings Catalogue, and
Washington Matthew's "The Night Chant, a Navaho Ceremony,"
Memoirs of the American Museum of Natural History, Vol.
VI. (May, 1902).

Songs performed are mainly from the Navaho Night Chant
ceremony and the Mountain Chant ceremony. The performers'
names are seldom given.

An additional one hundred cylinders recorded by Matthews
are held by the American Folklife Center at the Library of
Congress.

54-126-F. George Herzog, 1927.
    United States
        Pima Indians
            Arizona, Sacaton
                Corn ceremonies; Dance songs; Doctors' songs;
                Game songs; Healing songs; Hunting songs; Love
                songs[?]; Lullabies; Medicine songs; Myth songs;
                Puberty rites (female); Rain songs; Rites and
                ceremonies; Scalp songs; Unknown subjects;
                Victory songs; War songs

Number of cylinders: 41
Number of strips: 59
Sound quality of strips: EX 2,   G 34,   F 14,   P 9.
Degree of restriction: 2

All cylinders in this collection were recorded at the
Gila River Indian Reservation. There is one informant for
all of the songs, Thomas Vanyiko, a seventy year old Pima
Indian.
The Archives holds the original transcriptions of the
recordings found in this collection and Dr. Herzog's
extensive notes on Pima music, language, and ethnography.
A number of transciptions appear in the Journal of
American Folklore: Herzog, George, "A Comparison of Pueblo
and Pima Musical Styles." Vol. 49, No. 194 (1936), pp.
283-417.
A related collection is 54-228-F, recorded during
Herzog's second Pima field trip in 1929.

54-127-F. Livingston Farrand, 1898.
   United States
      Quileute Indians
         Washington, Granville [Pt. Grenville?]
            Unknown subjects

Number of cylinders: 10
Number of strips: 20
Sound quality of strips: P 16,   VP 4.
Degree of restriction: 2

Farrand recorded the Quileute and Quinault on an early
field trip to the state of Washington. (See 54-128-F.)
This is a small but complete collection. There is one
informant, Eunice, for all items. The song performances
are numbered, but no titles or genres are indicated.

54-128-F. Livingston Farrand, 1898.
   United States
      Quinault Indians
         Washington, Granville [Pt. Grenville?]
            Unknown subjects

Number of cylinders: 34
Number of strips: 68
Sound quality of strips: G 1,   P 57,   VP 10.
Degree of restriction: 2

This complete collection contains songs by informants
identified as Liza, Jesse, Lucy, and Jim Cape. There are
no title or genre designations.
The researcher might wish to consult Farrand's study of
the Quinault, "Traditions of the Quinault Indians."
Memoirs of the American Museum of Natural History, The
Jesup North Pacific Expedition, Vol. 4, 1900-09.

Related collection: 54-127-F   Farrand, Quileute Indians.

54-129-F. George Herzog, 1927.
   United States
      San Ildefonso Indians
         New Mexico, Sante Fe
            Sun dance songs

Number of cylinders: 2
Number of strips: 5
Sound quality of strips: F 1, B 4.
Degree of restriction: 2

   This collection contains two sun dance songs (one
incomplete), sung by Antonio Peña. Peña also sang the
second, third, and fourth songs of the eagle dance at this
time, which Herzog transcribed, but did not record.
Transcriptions of the eagle dance songs and the sun dance
songs may be found with this collection.
   Transcriptions of the sun dance songs appeared in Evans,
Bessie and May G., American Indian Dance Steps, 1931.

54-130-F. Thelma Adamson, 1927.
   United States
      Chehalis Indians
         Washington, Oakville, Chehalis Reservation
            Children's songs; Doctors' songs; Game songs;
            Love songs; Lullabies; Mythology; Snake songs;
            Spirit songs; Unknown subjects; War songs

Number of cylinders: 18
Number of strips: 31
Sound quality of strips: F 30, P 1.
Degree of restriction: 2

   This collection of songs and stories, as well as the
recordings under accession numbers 54-131-F (Adamson and
Boas), and 54-133-F (Adamson and Jacobs), were recorded
during the summer of 1927 on an AMNH-sponsored field trip
led by Franz Boas.
   The informants for this collection are Mr. and Mrs. Dan
Secena, Marion Davis, and Jonas Xwan, son of Dan Secena.
They perform, among others, songs described as "just a
song" and a song about a woman deserting a Scotsman. The
collector's inscriptions on the cylinder boxes have
provided the primary documentation.

54-131-F. Thelma Adamson and Franz Boas, 1927.
   United States
      Chehalis Indians
         Washington, Oakville, Chehalis Reservation
            Bear songs; Chants; Chiefs' songs; Deer songs;

Doctors' songs; Gambling songs; Love songs;
Lullabies; Marriage rites and ceremonies; Moon
songs; Mythology; Shamans' songs; Spirit songs;
Stories, narratives and anecdotes; Unknown
subjects
  Chehalis Indians (inf.); Nisqualli Indians (item)
    Washington, Oakville, Chehalis Reservation
    Chants; Gambling songs; Myths songs

Number of cylinders: 19
Number of strips: 30
Sound quality of strips: F 24,   P 6.
Degree of restriction: 2

   The documentation for this collection was prepared from
Franz Boas' inscriptions on the cylinder boxes and from
the American Museum of Natural History Phonorecordings
Catalogue. The single informant, Marion Davis, performs a
wide variety of songs.
   Transcriptions by George Herzog of ten cylinders
containing myth songs appeared in Adamson's article,
"Folk-Tales of the Coast Salish," Memoirs of the American
Folk-Lore Society, Vol. 27 (1934) pp. 422-30. Herzog's
original transcriptions of music and texts to the
published songs may be consulted as part of the
documentation.

Related collections: 54-130-F, and 54-133-F.

54-132-F.   Herman Karl Haeberlin, ca. 1917.
  United States
   Salish Indians
    Washington, Puget Sound District
     Gambling songs; Medicine songs; Unknown subjects;
     Women's songs
   Salish Indians (inf.); Snohomish Indians (item)
    Washington, Puget Sound District
     Love songs

Number of cylinders: 6
Number of strips: 10
Sound quality of strips: G 3,   F 7.
Degree of restriction: 2

   The documentation for these recordings consists of a
general place name and descriptions of the songs. The
performers' names are not given.
   All of the cylinders in this collection are mentioned in
the following publication: Roberts, Helen H. and Herman
K. Haeberlin. "Some Songs of the Puget Sound Salish."
Journal of American Folklore, Vol. 31 (1918),
pp. 498-518.

54-133-F. Melville Jacobs and Thelma Adamson, 1927.
    United States
      Cowlitz Indians
        Washington, Nesika
          Gambling songs; Humorous songs; Love songs;
          Meeting songs; Myth songs; Personal songs
      Cowlitz Indians (inf.); Taidnapam Indians (item)
        Washington, Nesika
          Gathering songs; Humorous songs; Lullabies;
          Meeting songs; Personal songs; Work songs
      Klikitat Indians
        Washington, Nesika
          Dance songs; Feast songs; Gathering songs;
          Humorous songs; Love songs; Myth songs; Personal
          songs
      Klikitat Indians (inf.); Chinook Indians (item)
        Washington, Nesika
          Love songs
      Klikitat Indians (inf.); Klamath Indians (item)
        Washington, Nesika
          Unknown subjects
      Klikitat Indians (inf.); Molala Indians (item)
        Washington, Nesika
          Love songs
      Klikitat Indians (inf.); Yakima Indians (item)
        Washington, Nesika
          War songs
      Yakima Indians
        Washington, Nesika
          Gambling songs; War songs
      Yakima Indians (inf.); Taidnapam Indians (item)
        Washington, Nesika
          Medicine songs; Meeting songs

Number of cylinders: 38
Number of strips: 57
Sound quality of strips: G 45, F 2, P 10.
Degree of restriction: 2

    These recordings were collected on a field trip
sponsored by the American Museum of Natural History.
Documentation was compiled from the AMNH Phonorecordings
Catalogue, inscriptions on the cylinder boxes, and notes
found inside the cylinder boxes.
    The informants are Sam Eyley, a Yakima Indian in his
eighties or nineties at the time of recording, Mrs. Sam
Eyley, a Cowlitz Indian about sixty-five years old, Mrs.
Mary Hunt, about ninety years old, a Klikitat Indian, and
Joe Hunt, a Klikitat medicine man assumed to be in his
eighties or nineties.

54-134-F. George Herzog, 1927.
    United States
      San Juan Indians
        Arizona, Sacaton

        Butterfly dance songs; Corn songs; Eagle dance
        songs; Humorous songs; Love songs; Round dance
        songs; Stories, narratives and anecdotes; War
        songs
    New Mexico, San Juan Pueblo
        Buffalo dance songs; Boys' dance songs;
        Children's songs; Corn dance songs; Dance songs;
        Dog dance songs; Eagle dance songs; Love songs;
        Meeting songs; Personal songs; Spring songs;
        Victory songs; War dance songs; War songs
San Juan Indians (inf.); Cheyenne Indians (item)
    New Mexico, San Juan Pueblo
        Round dance songs
San Juan Indians (inf.); Comanche Indians (item)
    New Mexico, San Juan Pueblo
        Dance songs
San Juan Indians (inf.); Jicarilla Indians (item)
    New Mexico, San Juan Pueblo
        Dance songs
San Juan Indians (inf.); Kiowa Indians (item)
    New Mexico, San Juan Pueblo
        Dance songs; Drinking songs
San Juan Indians (inf.); Pakana'wo Indians [?] (item)
    New Mexico, San Juan Pueblo
        Unknown subjects

Number of cylinders: 35
Number of strips: 50
Sound quality of strips: EX 35,   G 12,   F 3.
Degree of restriction: 2

   George Herzog recorded these cylinders on an expedition
sponsored by the American Museum of Natural History. His
field notes and text and music transcriptions of nearly
all the cylinders supplement the documentation to this
collection. Two of the cylinders in this collection were
transcribed by Dr. Herzog and are included in "A
Comparison of Pueblo and Pima Musical Styles," The Journal
of American Folklore, Vol, 49, No. 194 (1936), pp. 283-
417.
   Five men of ages ranging from twenty-six to seventy-two
are the individual singers.

54-135-F. Herbert Joseph Spinden, 1912.
   United States
    Nambé Indians
      New Mexico, Nambé
        Corn dance songs; Initiation rites; Snake dance
        songs; Turtle dance songs; Women's dance songs[?]
    Santa Clara Indians
      New Mexico, Santa Clara Indian Reservation
        Dance songs; Harvest dance songs; Turtle dance
        songs; War dance songs; Women's dance songs
    Nambé Indians (inf.); Comanche Indians[?] (item)
      New Mexico, Nambé Pueblo

Elk dance songs

Number of cylinders: 12
Number of strips: 13
Sound quality of strips: G 1, F 11, VP 1.
Degree of restriction: 2

This is a small but complete collection of cylinders. Announcements on the cylinders give the name and place of the performance. No performer's names are given. George Herzog's transcription of one war dance song is included in the documentation.
The collector has published an article which gives photographic and general narrative coverage of the Pueblo Indians, which may be of comparative value: Spinden, Herbert J. "Indian Dances of the Southwest," American Museum Journal, Vol. 15, 1915, pp. 103-115.

54-136-F. Pliny Earle Goddard, ca. 1905.
    Canada
        Sarsi Indians
            Alberta, Sarcee Indian Reservation
                Dance songs; Feast songs; Gambling songs; Game songs; Pipe songs; Sacred songs; Sun dance songs; Tea dance songs; Thunder songs; Unknown subjects; War songs

Number of cylinders: 26
Number of strips: 33
Sound quality of strips: F 22, P 8, VP 3.
Degree of restriction: 2

Goddard collected these songs as part of his ethnographic research for the American Museum of Natural History. The AMNH Phonograph Recordings Catalogue lists specimen markers for nine songs recorded by Goddard.
The names for the informants for this collection, where mentioned, were found inscribed on the original cylinder boxes or were written on slips of paper tucked inside of the cylinders. They are Brow Leather, Grasshopper, and Jack Head Above Water.

54-137-F. George Herzog, 1927.
    United States
        Serrano Indians
            California, Morongo Reservation, Banning
                Bear songs; Children's songs; Dance songs; Doctors' songs; Funeral rites and ceremonies; Game songs; Laments; Lullabies; Rites and ceremonies; Shamans' songs; Stories, narratives and anecdotes (songs from); War dance songs

Number of cylinders: 13
Number of strips: 18
Sound quality of strips: F 10,   P 8.
Degree of restriction: 2

    Rose Morongo, an eighty-year-old woman of Cahuilla
descent, is the sole performer for this complete
collection recorded for the American Museum of Natural
History. George Herzog's music and text transcriptions
for all cylinders supplement the documentation.

54-138-F. George Herzog, 1927.
    United States
      Taos Indians
        New Mexico, Taos Pueblo
          Boys' dance songs; Buffalo dance songs; Corn
          dance songs; Dance songs; Deer dance songs; Eagle
          dance songs; Flower dance songs; Game songs; Gift
          distribution dance songs; Humorous songs; Love
          songs; Medicine songs; Pumpkin dance songs; Rites
          and ceremonies; Squaw dance songs; Sun dance
          songs; Turtle dance songs; War dance songs;
          Women's dance songs; Women's songs
      Taos Indians (inf.) Cheyenne Indians (item)
        New Mexico, Taos Pueblo
          Squaw dance songs
      Taos Indians (inf.); Zuñi Indians (item)
        New York, New York City
          Unknown subjects

Number of cylinders: 28
Number of strips: 48
Sound quality of strips: G 12,   F 33,   P 3.
Degree of restriction: 2

    This collection contains twenty-five cylinders recorded
at the Taos Pueblo and three recorded in New York City.
The informants are Sam Martínez, his aunt (unnamed),
and Antonio Lujan, also known as Tony Luhan. Their
recordings feature a variety of dance songs. One dance
for giving things away includes a song for the giver and a
song for the receiver.
    Herzog's transcriptions of music and song texts and his
field notes are part of the documentation to the New
Mexico group of recordings.

Reference:
Herzog, George. "A Comparison of Pueblo and Pima Musical
Styles," Journal of American Folklore, Vol. 49, No. 194
(1936), pp. 283-417.

Related collection: 83-900-F

54-139-F.   Franz Boas and James Alexander Teit, 1897.
   Canada
      Ntlakyapamuk Indians
         British Columbia, Spence's Bridge
            Bear songs; Dance songs; Gambling songs; Medicine
            songs; Men's songs; Potlatch songs; Prayers;
            Sacred dance songs; Sacred songs; Unknown
            subjects; Women's songs

Number of cylinders: 44
Number of strips: 46
Sound quality of strips: F 5,   P 9,   VP 29,   B 2,   U 1.
Degree of restriction: 2

   These cylinders are galvano-plastic copies of the
original field recordings.
   All of the recordings were made at Spence's Bridge, a
town near the junction of the Thompson and Nicola rivers,
British Columbia. Franz Boas, working as a part of the
famous Jesup North Pacific Expedition, was aided by James
Teit, a Scotsman who had married a Thompson River Indian
woman and became conversant in the local dialect. Teit
became a guide, primary assistant, and co-author with Boas
for scholarly accounts of the Thompson River culture.
   The documentation for this collection has come primarily
from the American Museum of Natural History
Phonorecordings Catalogue. The original cylinder boxes
contain no information. Informants are not named and the
songs are given very general identifications.

54-140-F.   Paul Radin, 1908.
   United States
      British Americans
         Nebraska, Winnebago Indian Reservation
            Unknown subjects
      British Americans (item)
         Nebraska, Winnebago Indian Reservation
            Humorous songs
      French[?]
         Nebraska, Winnebago Indian Reservation
            Unknown subjects
      Oto Indians (item)
         Nebraska, Winnebago Indian Reservation
            Unknown subjects
      Potawatomi Indians (item)
         Nebraska, Winnebago Indian Reservation
            Unknown subjects
      Winnebago Indians
         Nebraska, Winnebago Indian Reservation
            Buffalo dance songs; Flute music; Guessing game
            songs; Love songs; Mescal songs; Moccasin songs;
            Soldiers' songs; Stories, narratives and
            anecdotes; Unknown subjects
      Winnebago Indians (inf.); Chippewa Indians (item)
         Nebraska, Winnebago Indian Reservation

          Unknown subjects
     Winnebago Indians (inf.); Crow Indians (item)
       Nebraska, Winnebago Indian Reservation
          Unknown subjects
     Winnebago Indians (inf.); Dakota Indians (item)
       Nebraska, Winnebago Indian Reservation
          Unknown subjects
     Winnebago Indians (inf.); Omaha Indians (item)
       Nebraska, Winnebago Indian Reservation
          Unknown subjects
     Winnebago Indians (inf.); Oto Indians (item)
       Nebraska, Winnebago Indian Reservation
          Unknown subjects
     Winnebago Indians (inf.); Ponca Indians (item)
       Nebraska, Winnebago Indian Reservation
          Unknown subjects
     Winnebago Indians (item)
       Nebraska, Winnebago Indian Reservation
          Victory songs

Number of cylinders: 56
Number of strips: 60
Sound quality of strips: EX 3, G 39, F 17, P 1.
Degree of restriction: 2

    This is a complete collection of cylinders.
Documentation for this collection was compiled from
cylinder box inscriptions, George Herzog's worknotes and
from information found on the cylinder recordings
themselves. The seven informants, all male, provide songs
from a variety of culture groups for this collection.

54-141-F. Frank Gouldsmith Speck, ca. 1905.
     United States
       Creek Indians
         Oklahoma, Taskigi [Tuskegee?]
           Dance songs; Medicine songs; Owl dance songs
       Yuchi Indians
         Oklahoma, Taskigi [Tuskegee?]
           Dance songs; Flute music; Game songs; Horse dance
           songs; Round dance songs; Stories, narratives and
           anecdotes; Turtle dance songs
       Yuchi Indians, Chickasaw Indians and Shawnee Indians
         Oklahoma, Taskigi [Tuskegee?]
           Rain songs
     [United States]
       Creek Indians
         [Oklahoma, Tuskegee?]
           Owl dance songs
       Unknown culture groups
         [Oklahoma, Tuskegee?]
           Mythology; Stories, narratives and anecdotes;
           Unknown subjects

Number of cylinders: 17

Number of strips: 23
Sound quality of strips: F 7, P 3, VP 13.
Degree of restriction: 2

   This group of cylinders, along with those in 54-107-F,
form what appears to be a complete collection.
   The following publication adds great research value to
this collection: Speck, Frank G. Ceremonial Songs of the
Creek and Yuchi Indians. University of Pennsylvania,
Anthropological Publications, Vol I, No. 2, Philadelphia,
1911. This volume contains Jacob Sapir's music
transcriptions of specific cylinders in 54-141-F and
54-107-F.

54-142-F. George Herzog, 1927.
   United States
      Yuma Indians
         Arizona, Yuma
            Game songs; Unknown subjects

Number of cylinders: 24
Number of strips: 25
Sound quality of strips: G 21, F 2, P 2.
Degree of restriction: 2

   An article by the collector gives valuable information
about these cylinders, including transcriptions of the
melodies: "The Yuman Musical Style." Journal of American
Folklore, Vol. 41, No. 160 (1928), pp. 183-231. All
cylinders contain the songs of one man, Frank Hills. He
performs excerpts from song cyles: birds song cycle,
Harra'up song cycle, and frog song cycle. He also sings
guessing game songs (also called Peon game songs).
Several of the songs have a percussion accompaniment.
   George Herzog's original text and music transcriptions
supplement the documentation to the collection.

54-143-F. Elsie Worthington Clews Parsons [?], 1925 [?].
   United States
      Zuñi Indians
         Unknown locations
            Unknown subjects

Number of cylinders: 1
Number of strips: 1
Sound quality of strips: F 1.
Degree of restriction: 2

   The AMNH Catalogue gives this information about the
cylinder: "Songs probably recorded by Mrs. E.C. Parsons
from Shorty. a) Shumaki; b) Upi Kyayapona songs (foreign);
c) duplicate of "b".

54-144-F. George Herzog, 1927.
     United States
       Zuñi Indians
         New Mexico, Gallup, Zuñi Pueblo
           Buffalo dance songs; Dance songs; Gambling songs;
           Game songs; Grinding songs; Initiation rites;
           Kachinas; Medicine songs; Rain dance songs; Rites
           and ceremonies; Society songs; Unknown subjects;
           War songs

Number of cylinders: 23
Number of strips: 34
Sound quality of strips: EX 1, G 11, F 22.
Degree of restriction: 2

   The same informant, Nick, is listed for all 23 cylinders
in this collection.
   Herzog's music and text transcriptions and his field
notes supplement the documentation to this collection. Six
of the transcriptions were published in Herzog, George. "A
Comparison of Pueblo and Pima Musical Styles," Journal of
American Folklore, Vol. 49, No. 194. (1036), pp. 283-417.
   A few of the recordings include a pitch ("A"), which is
helpful for determining playback speed.

54-145-F. Natalie Curtis Burlin, ca. 1917.
     United States
       Afro-Americans
         Virginia, Hampton
           Folk-songs; Gospel music; Unknown subjects

Number of cylinders: 15
Number of strips: 15
Sound quality of strips: EX 2, G 1, F 10, P 1, B 1.
Degree of restriction: 2

   Although Natalie Curtis Burlin is known primarily for
her work among North American Indians, she also recorded
this small but extremely valuable collection of Afro-
American songs and spirituals. Recorded at the Hampton
Institute, in Virginia, these cylinders represent an
important sample of Afro-American music as it was actually
performed in the early part of the twentieth century. All
of the gospel songs are sung by the Hampton Quartette, a
self-organized and self-trained male quartet which
performed in and around the Hampton Institute. Some of
these songs, such as "listen to de Lambs," and "'Tis me, O
Lord," were transcribed by Mrs. Burlin for her
publication, Hampton Series Negro Folk-Songs, Books I-IV.
New York: G. Schirmer, C. 1918-1919.

Reference:
Smith, Ronald R. "Natalie Curtis Burlin at the Hampton
Institute," Resound, Vol. I, No. 2 (April, 1982), pp. 1-2.

54-146-F.   Helen Heffron Roberts or Elsie Worthington
            Clews Parsons [?], ca. 1920.
   [Jamaica?]
      Unknown culture groups
         Unknown locations
            Drinking songs

Number of cylinders: 1
Number of strips: 1
Sound quality of strips: F 1.
Degree of restriction: 2

   The American Museum of Natural History Phonorecordings
Catalogue gives the following information regarding this
one cylinder: "West Indian Negro - Two songs, the first
bad. Probably Mrs. E.C. Parsons or Miss Helen Roberts."
The recording itself, however, is not a West Indian Negro
song; it is a hearty performance of an English drinking
song, "More Ale," by an unidentified male singer.

54-147-F.   Martha Warren Beckwith and Helen Heffron
            Roberts, 1921.
   Jamaica
      Jamaicans
         Brownstown
            Flute music
         [Brownstown]
            Flute music
         Christiania
            Polkas; Unknown subjects
         Laconia
            Flute music; Unknown subjects
         Maroon Town
            Drinking songs; Funeral rites and ceremonies;
            Game songs; Sailors' songs; Stories, narratives
            and anecdotes (songs from); Unknown subjects
         Prospect, Watson's Hill
            Hymns; Unknown subjects
         Trysee[?]
            Flute music

Number of cylinders: 72
Number of strips: 90
Sound quality of strips: G 9, F 18, P 46, VP 16, B 1.
Degree of restriction: 2

   This is a complete collection; the first fifteen
cylinders were recorded by Helen Roberts and the last
fifty-seven cylinders were recorded by Martha Beckwith.
There is a great number of informants, and there is good
variety in the types of songs performed.

54-148-F.   John Alden Mason, 1914-1915.
    Puerto Rico
       Puerto Ricans
          Unknown locations
             Aguinaldos; Bombas; Coplas; Corridos; Dance
             music; Dance songs; Decimas; Festival songs; Game
             songs; Guarachas; Instrumental music;
             Malagueñas; Mazurkas; Polkas; Rumbas;
             Sigurillas; Stories, narratives and anecdotes
             (songs from); Tangos; Tumalitas; Unknown
             subjects; Waltzes

Number of cylinders: 174
Number of strips: 322
Sound quality of strips: EX 96,   G 124,   F 50,   P 27,
        VP 17, B 8.
Degree of restriction: 2

   This collection appears to be complete. Not all
informants are listed, but more than a dozen names appear
in the documentation, which has been derived mainly from
inscriptions on the original cylinder boxes.

Reference:
Alegria, Ricardo E. "The Fiesta of Santiago Apostol in
Loize, Puerto Rico." Journal of American Folklore, Vol.
69, No. 272 (1956), pp. 123-34.

54-149-F.   Waldemar Bogoras and Waldemar Jochelson, 1901-
           1902.
    Soviet Union
       Chukchi
          [Siberia]
             Shamans' songs; Unknown subjects
          Siberia, Marinsky Post
             Men's songs; Shamans' songs; Stories, narratives
             and anecdotes; Throat rattling; Unknown subjects;
             Women's songs
       Eskimos
          [Siberia]
             Unknown subjects
       Koryaks
          Siberia, Chaibugn River
             Shamans' songs
          Siberia, Itkana
             Stories, narratives and anecdotes
          Siberia, Karoenskoye
             Shamans' songs; Stories, narratives and
             anecdotes; Unknown subjects
          Siberia, Kuel [Lake]
             Shamans' songs; Stories, narratives and
             anecdotes; Unknown subjects
          Siberia, Uterskaya Kuel
             Shamans' songs
       Koryaks[?]

      Siberia, Marinsky Post
        Unknown subjects
    Koryaks (inf.); Chukchi (item)
      Siberia, Opuka, Kamenskoe
        Unknown subjects
    Russians
      [Siberia]
        Marriage rites and ceremonies
      Siberia, Kolyma River, Yakutskaya
        Dance songs; Marriage rites and ceremonies;
        Unknown subjects
      Siberia, Magadanskaya, Marcova
        Carols; Epics; Instrumental music; Love songs;
        Ring dance songs; Unknown subjects
      Siberia, Marinsky Post
        Carols; Dance songs; Epics; Love songs; Ring
        dance songs; Sailors' songs; Unknown subjects
    Tunguses
      [Siberia]
        Shamans' songs; Stories, narratives and
        anecdotes, (songs from)
      Siberia, Indian Point
        Shamans' songs; Love songs; Unknown subjects
      Siberia, Kolyma River, Yakutskaya
        Shamans' songs
      Siberia, Marinsky Post
        Unknown subjects
      Siberia, Najachon
        Shamans' songs; Stories, narratives and anecdotes
      Unknown locations
        Shamans' songs
    Unknown culture groups
      [Siberia]
        Shamans' songs; Unknown subjects
      Siberia, Magadanskaya, Marcova
        Unknown subjects
    Yakuts
      Siberia, Yakutskaya
        Shamans' songs; Spirit songs; Stories, narratives
        and anecdotes
      Siberia, Yakutskaya, Kolyma River
        Stories, narratives and anecdotes; Unknown
        subjects
    Yukaghir
      Siberia, Kolyma River, Yakutskaya
        Unknown subjects
      Siberia, Magadanskaya, Yassachnojo River
        Shamans' songs; Stories, narratives and anecdotes

Number of cylinders: 137
Number of strips: 204
Sound quality of strips: EX 5, G 24, F 150, P 19,
    VP 3, B 3.
Degree of restriction: 2

This collection was recorded as a part of the Jesup
North Pacific Expedition sponsored by the American Museum
of Natural History. Despite numerous physical hardships,
the two ethnographers, travelling in different areas of
arctic Siberia, were able to collect thousands of
ethnographical items, including wax cylinder recordings.
    The Cylinder Project received assistance in documenting
this collection from Andrew Durkin of the Slavics
Department, Indiana University, who translated the
inscriptions on the original cylinder boxes into English.

Related collection: 80-226-F. Waldemar Jochelson, North
America, U.S., Alaska, Aleutian Islands, Eskimo, 1909-11.)

Reference:
Boas, Franz, "The Jesup North Pacific Expedition," The
American Museum Journal, Vol. III, No. 5, October 1903.
This article includes accounts of the expedition written
by both Bogoras and Jochelson.

54-150-F.   Berthold Laufer, 1901-1902.
    China
      Chinese
        Peking
          Brothel songs; Flower songs[?]; Game songs;
          Laments; Love songs; Marriage rites and
          ceremonies; Music, Popular ; Opium songs; Rites
          and ceremonies; Theater music; Unknown subjects
        [Peking]
          Unknown subjects
        Shanghai
          Brothel songs[?]; Horse songs[?]; Instrumental
          music; Shepherds' songs; Star ceremonies[?];
          Theater music; Unknown subjects
      Unknown culture groups
        Shanghai
          Unknown subjects

Number of cylinders: 400
Number of strips: 401
Sound quality of strips: EX 38, G 140, F 156, P 51,
        VP 5, B 11.
Degree of restriction: 2

    Sponsored by the American Museum of Natural History,
Laufer led the Jacob H. Schiff Expedition to China between
the years 1901 and 1904. The object of the expedition was
to document the "complete culture" of China. The
cylinders which Laufer recorded represent Chinese drama,
art songs, and Shadow Play music of that period. Many are
vocal songs, with a rich instrumental accompaniment, and
some are strictly instrumental compositions. The
instruments recorded include flutes, fiddles, lutes,
gongs, single and double reed aerophones, bells, and

membranophones. Although many of the cylinders are marred
by bad tracking and surface mold, some are of good quality
and have produced an excellent sound. In these cases, the
sound is so clear that the listener feels as though he is
listening to a live performance.
    Michael Welsh of the Indiana University Library
translated the archaic Chinese characters in the original
catalogue in order to provide completely revised
documentation for this collection.

References:
Graf, Marilyn, "The Chinese Collection of Dr. Berthold
Laufer." Resound, Vol. 1, No. 2, pp. 3-4, April, 1982.

Walravens, Hartmut, ed. Keinere Schriften von Bertold
Laufer. 2 vols. Wiesbaden: Franz Steiner Verlag, 1976;
1979.

54-152-F. James Francis Hurley, 1921.
    New Guinea
        Unknown culture groups
            Unknown locations
                Dance songs

Number of cylinders: 7
Number of strips: 11
Sound quality of strips: G 5, F 3, VP 3.
Degree of restriction: 2

    This collection originally held 9 cylinders; two are now
missing. The expedition which produced these recordings
was led by a traveller and adventurer, Captain Frank
Hurley, who wrote a book in diary form, Pearls and Savages
(New York: G.P. Putman and Sons, 1924), to document his
findings. The following discussion of the recording
session might be of interest to any field worker:
    "It was with the greatest difficulty that these
    could be made to understand what a phonograph was and
    that it was necessary to stand before it and sing
    directly into the horn in order to secure the proper
    results.
    "All efforts at precision failed until a record was
    made in the rough and then played for the benefit of
    the group. Instantly they understood, and from then
    on the recording was a simple matter. They began at
    the right moment, sang perfectly in unison, and
    finished at a given signal." (p. 172)
The only descriptions of these performances are "songs and
dances." Most are accompanied by a drum. Some are solo
and some are group performances. Singing seems to have
been done mainly by men.

54-181-F. Charles Frederick and Erminie Wheeler-Voegelin,
          1935.
  United States
    Shawnee Indians
      Oklahoma, Shawnee
        Bean dance songs; Bear dance songs; Bread dance
        songs; Buffalo dance songs; Corn dance songs;
        Dance songs; Drinking dance songs; Drinking
        songs; Evening songs; Gourd dance songs;
        Invectives and derisions; Love songs; Lullabies;
        Meeting songs; Mocassin dance songs; Night dance
        songs; Night songs; Peyote songs; Pumpkin dance
        songs; Social dance songs; Stories, narratives
        and anecdotes (songs from); Unknown subjects;
        Women's dance songs

Number of cylinders: 50
Number of strips: 61
Sound quality of strips: G 18, F 36, P 6, VP 1.
Degree of restriction: 2

   Erminie Wheeler-Voegelin apparently conducted most of
the research for this collection. The documentation is
complete; all cylinders contain the location of the
recording, the name of the informant, the date of the
recording, and the title of the song or story. The
cylinder recordings themselves also supply the listener,
with the stabilizing sound of three pitches, A-E-A, at the
beginning of each performance.
   The Archives of Traditional Music also holds
transcriptions for five of the Shawnee songs in this
collection. They were made by Bruno Nettl, ca. 1951.

54-185-F. Melville Jacobs, 1929-1930.
  United States
    Clackamas Indians
      Oregon, Oregon City and West Linn
        Bear power songs; Chipmunk power songs; Coyote
        songs; Dance songs; Doctors' songs; Earth power
        songs; Fire power songs; Fog power songs;
        Gambling songs; Hand game songs; Humorous
        songs[?]; Laments; Love songs[?]; Lullabies;
        Mouse power songs; Mythology; Owl power songs;
        Personal songs; Power songs; Rabbit power songs;
        Snake power songs; Songs for the dead; Spirit
        songs; Sturgeon power songs; Sunset power songs
    Clackamas Indians (inf.); Kalapuyan Indians (item)
      Oregon
        Doctors' songs; Power songs; Shamans' songs;
        Thunder power songs[?]
    Clackamas Indians (inf.); Klamath Indians [?] (item)
      Oregon
        Sunset power songs
    Clackamas Indians (inf.); Molala Indians (item)
      Oregon, Oregon City and West Linn

                   Blood power songs; Coyote power songs; Dawn power
                   songs; Hand game songs; Power songs; Puberty
                   rites (female); Shamans' songs; Snake power songs
            Clackamas Indians (inf.); Shasta Indians [?] (item)
               Oregon, West Linn
               Dance songs
            Clackamas Indians (inf.); Shoshoni Indians (item)
               Oregon, Oregon City
               Spider power songs

Number of cylinders: 26
Number of strips: 109
Sound quality of strips: G 50, F 53, P 6.
Degree of restriction: 3

   The principal informant for this collection is Mrs.
Victoria Howard, a Clackamas Chinook, recorded at West
Linn, Oregon. The recordings indicate that there may be
at least three other singers, whose names are unknown.
   Mrs. Howard performs numerous power songs, many of which
are power songs of her male and female relatives. A large
number of songs are sung in dialects extinct at the time
of recording.
   The documentation includes a complete set of music and
text transcriptions prepared by George Herzog.

54-191-F. Willard Zerbe Park, 1934.
     United States
        Paiute Indians
           Unknown locations
              Antelope dance songs; Dance songs; Doctor's
              songs; Hand game songs; Round dance songs;
              Women's songs

Number of cylinders: 10
Number of strips: 16
Sound quality of strips: F 2, P 14.
Degree of restriction: 1

   Most of these cylinder recordings contain English
announcements which give the name of the informant, the
home city of the informant, and the title of the song
performed.
   Willard Z. Park's field notes to this collection may be
found at the Getchell Library at the University of Nevada,
Reno.
   The sound quality of the cylinders is seriously impaired
by wildly fluctuating recording speeds.

54-192-F. George A. Dorsey and James R. Murie, ca. 1905.
     United States
        Pawnee Indians
           Unknown locations
              Bear songs; Coyote songs[?]; Medicine bundle

                   songs; Stories, narratives and anecdotes; Unknown
                   subjects
            Pawnee Indians[?]
               Unknown locations
               Unknown subjects

Number of cylinders: 224
Number of strips: 224
Sound quality of strips: G 1,   F 86,   P 35,   VP 90,
         B 11, U 1.
Degree of restriction: 2

   These cylinders were originally deposited at the the
Field Museum of Natural History in Chicago. Although
often referred to as the Dorsey collection, Murie's name
should also be included. Murie was a Pawnee ethnographer
who worked both for Dorsey and for the Bureau of American
Ethnology in Washington, D.C.
   Many of the cylinders contain recordings of narratives:
star lore, life histories, animal spirit stories, stories
of the origins of dances, or stories about ethics, work,
and burial. There are very few songs.
   It is unfortunate that many of these cylinders are of
poor or very poor sound quality. Over the years, an
accumulation of mold destroyed the cylinder grooves to the
extent that almost no signal can be heard.
   The researcher may be aided by the following reference:
Murie, James R. Ceremonies of the Pawnee, Pt. I, II.
Parks, Douglas R., ed. Smithsonian Contributions to
Anthropology, No. 27, Washington, D.C.: Smithsonian Press,
1981.

54-196-F. Milford G. Chandler, ca. 1926.
      United States
         Winnebago Indians
            Unknown locations
               Stories, narratives and anecdotes

Number of cylinders: 90
Number of strips: 91
Sound quality of strips: F 29,   P 46,   B 16.
Degree of restriction: 3

   This collection, apparently complete, has an interesting
history. In 1959, more than thirty years after the
initial fieldwork, a researcher named Gerd Fraenkel took
copies of some of Chandler's recordings back to Winnebago
Indians, in Black River Falls, Wisconsin, and played them.
After listening to the stories on the tapes, the Indians
retold the stories to Fraenkel. These retold stories may
be found in the Archives of Traditional Music under
accession number 59-059-F.

54-206-F. Helen Heffron Roberts, 1923.
    United States
        Hawaiians
            Hawaii, Kauai
                Unknown subjects

Number of cylinders: 5
Number of strips: 9
Sound quality of strips: G 1, F 4, P 4.
Degree of restriction: 3

   The greater portion of this collection is held by the
Bernice P. Bishop Museum in Honolulu. The documentation
for these cylinders has been compiled from inscriptions on
the original cylinder boxes and from information received
from the Bishop Museum.
 The singers, K. Paikulu, P.K. Kuhi, and Lucy
Kapohaialii, are unaccompanied.

54-210-F. Karl Edvard Laman, 1913-1922.
    Congo
        Bakongo (African people)
            Unknown locations
                Boat songs; Dance songs

Number of cylinders: 7
Number of strips: 7
Sound quality of strips: G 4, P 2, VP 1.
Degree of restriction: 1

   This collection, along with 54-211-F, represents a very
small portion of the cylinders recorded by Laman in the
Congo. These cylinders were loaned to George Herzog for
transcription, and transcriptions for nearly all of the
cylinders have been found among George Herzog's papers.
Numerous transcriptions of Laman's cylinders now housed at
the Berlin Phonogramm-Archiv are also available for
consultation.

References:
Laman, K. E. "The Musical Accent or Intonation in the
Kongo Language," Stockholm, 1922.

Jansen, John M. "Laman's Kongo Ethnography: Observations
on Sources, Methodology and Theory." Africa, Vol. 42
(1972), pp. 316-328.

Related collection: 54-211-F, Laman, French Equatorial
Africa, Bateke.

54-211-F. Karl Edvard Laman, 1913-1922.
    French Equatorial Africa
        Teke (African people)
            Unknown locations

Dance songs; Unknown subjects

Number of cylinders: 21
Number of strips: 21
Sound quality of strips: G 12, F 5, P 3, B 1.
Degree of restriction: 1

   This collection is incomplete and very little
documentation is available for the recordings. For the
most part, "dance song" is all that is given in terms of
performance description.
   The songs are sung by mixed groups and boy's choruses
with solo performers. Hand clapping is the accompaniment
in some cases, as is a chordophone in a few others. Music
transcriptions made by George Herzog may be consulted as
documentation for this collection.

Related collection: 54-210-F Laman, Congo, Bakongo.

54-223-F. George Herzog, 1930-1931.
   Liberia
      Jabo (African people)
         Nimiah
            Bird dance songs; Drum music; Eagle dance songs;
            Instrumental music; Owl dance songs; Prayer
            songs; Signals (drum); Signals (horn); Songs of
            honor and praise; Unknown subjects

Number of cylinders: 236
Number of strips: 411
Sound quality of strips: F 56, P 230, VP 122, B 2,
         U 1.
Degree of restriction: 1

   George Herzog recorded this large collection of
cylinders on an expedition sponsored by the University of
Chicago.
   Some cylinders contain recordings of horn playing and
horn signalling, for purposes ranging from the signal used
when a wild cow is killed to that which is sounded when
the body of a drowned person is discovered. This
collection includes a number of drum signalling
recordings; the uses of drum signals are also widely
varied. The xylophone pieces are often titled, and seem
to be used in connection with specific people or animals.
Finally, there is a group of songs, entitled "sweet mouth"
singing, which are unfortunately of poor fidelity.
   George Herzog's field notebooks, containing item-by-item
descriptions, and in many cases, transcriptions of the
recordings, provide valuable documentation for these
cylinders.

54-224-F. George Herzog, 1929[?].
    United States [?]
      Jabo [?] (African people)
        Illinois, Chicago [?]
          Unknown subjects

Number of cylinders: 1
Number of strips: 3
Sound quality of strips: P 3.
Degree of restriction: 1

    There is no reliable documentation for this cylinder.

54-228-F. George Herzog, 1929.
    United States
      Maricopa Indians
        Arizona, Sacaton, Gila River Indian Reservation
          Flute music; Myth songs
      Pima Indians
        Arizona, Sacaton, Gila River Indian Reservation
          Drinking songs; Bawdy songs; Flute songs; Myth
          songs
      Pima Indians (inf.); Maricopa Indians (item)
        Arizona, Sacaton, Gila River Indian Reservation
          Flute music; Myth songs

Number of cylinders: 116
Number of strips: 240
Sound quality of strips: G 16, F 198, P 26.
Degree of restriction: 1

    George Herzog recorded these cylinders in connection
with an investigation of the interrelationships of Pima
language, poetry, and music. The project was suggested by
Franz Boas and funded by Columbia University.
    Herzog's music and text transcriptions of these
recordings provide valuable documentation. In addition,
the collection contains a draft of an unpublished
manuscript on Pima myths for which the song transcriptions
and translations serve as illustrations. The manuscript
contains transcriptions of the myths. Dr. Herzog's notes
indicate that the songs were recorded as the stories were
being written down.
    Materials Herzog collected during the 1929 field trip,
in combination with recordings and data gathered in 1927,
1933, and 1936, formed the basis for several unpublished
studies of Pima myth, ethnology, and linguistics, all of
which may be found at the Archives of Traditional Music.
    The principal performer for this collection was Thomas
Vanyiko. Other performers were Albert James and Roy Azul,
who also acted as Herzog's translator.

Reference: Herzog, George. "A Comparison of Pueblo and
Pima Musical Styles," Journal of American Folklore Vol.
49, No. 194 (1936), pp. 283-417.

57-014-F.   Edward S. Curtis, 1907-1913.
    Canada
      Clayoquot Indians
        British Columbia, Vancouver Island, Clayoquot Sound
          Medicine songs; Prayers; Rejoicing songs; War
          songs; Whaling songs
      Cowichan Indians
        British Columbia, Juamichan[?]
          Love songs; Potlatch songs; Songs of thanks
      Haida Indians
        British Columbia, Queen Charlotte Islands,
        Skidegate
          Childrens' songs; Dance songs; Initation rites;
          Laments; Love songs; Mask songs; Rejoicing songs;
          Songs of honor and praise; Tattooing songs; War
          songs
      Hesquiat Indians [?]
        British Columbia, Vancouver Island, Clayoquot Sound
          Lullabies; Medicine songs; Women's songs
      Kwakiutl Indians
        British Columbia, Vancouver Island, Fort Rupert
          Bear songs; Childrens' songs; Healing songs; Love
          songs; Mask songs; Morning songs; Rites and
          ceremonies; Winter songs
    United States
      Arapaho Indians
        Wyoming, Arapaho, Wind River Indian Reservation
          Dance songs; Lodge songs; Love songs; Sun dance
          songs
      Atsina Indians
        Montana, Fort Belknap Indian Reservation
          Grass dance songs; Hand game songs; Humorous
          songs; Lodge songs; Lullabies; Medicine songs;
          Pipe songs; Society songs; Sun dance songs;
          Victory songs; War songs; War dance songs;
          Women's dance songs
      Cheyenne Indians
        Montana, Tongue River Indian Reservation
          Dance songs; Greeting songs; Lodge songs; Love
          songs; Scouts' songs; Society songs; Sun dance
          songs; War songs; Wolf songs
      Cochiti Indians
        New Mexico, Tesuque
          Healing songs; Medicine songs
      [Crow Indians?]
        Montana, Pryor, Crow Indian Reservation
          War songs
      Klikitat Indians
        Washington, Klickitat
          Dance songs; Gambling songs; Medicine songs
      Kutenai Indians
        Montana, Polson, Flathead Indian Reservation
          Bear songs; Deer songs; Hand game songs; Lodge
          songs; Love songs; Medicine songs; Rejoicing
          songs; Rites and ceremonies; Society songs; War
          songs

Nez Percé Indians
  Idaho, Ft. Lapwai, Lapwai Indian Reservation
    Animal imitations; Bear songs; Love songs;
    Medicine songs; Victory songs; War songs
Nez Percé Indians[?]
  Idaho, Ft. Lapwai, Lapwai Indian Reservation
    Songs of prophecy
Salish Indians
  Montana, Arlee, Flathead Indian Reservation
    Buffalo songs; Greeting songs; Healing songs [?];
    Love songs; Rejoicing songs; Scouts' songs; War
    dance songs; Women's songs
Shoshoni Indians
  Wyoming, Fort Washakie, Wind River Indian
  Reservation
    Bear dance songs; Dance songs; Ghost dance songs;
    Society songs; Sun dance songs; Tea dance songs;
    Victory songs; War dance songs; War songs
[Snohomish Indians?]
  Washington, Nespelem, Colville Indian Reservation
    Love songs; Medicine songs; Traveling songs; War
    songs
Unknown culture groups
  Montana, Poplar
    Buffalo songs; Love songs; Medicine songs; Night
    dance songs; Scalp dance songs; Speeches,
    addresses, etc.; Sun dance songs; War songs
  Montana, Pryor, Crow Indian Reservation
    Bear dance songs; Coyote songs; Dance songs; Dog
    songs; Fox songs; Lodge songs; Medicine songs;
    Mythology; Sacred songs; Sacrificial offerings;
    Scouts' songs; Society songs; Songs for the dead;
    Sun dance songs; Tobacco songs; Victory songs;
    War songs
  Montana, Wolf Point
    Hand game songs; Medicine songs; Songs of thanks;
    Sun dance songs; Tea dance songs
  New Mexico, San Ildefonso
    Buffalo dance songs; Eagle dance songs; Grinding
    songs; Marriage rites and ceremonies; Rain songs
  New Mexico, San Juan Pueblo
    Basket dance songs; Dance songs; Eagle dance
    songs; Rattle dance songs; Scalp dance songs;
    Turtle dance songs
  New Mexico, Tesuque
    Dance songs
  South Dakota, Pine Ridge
    Fox songs
  Washington, Nespelem, Colville Indian Reservation
    Nature songs
  Washington, Wishliam [Wishram?]
    Canoe songs; Courtship rites and ceremonies;
    Dance songs; Lodge songs; Love songs; Medicine
    songs; Songs for the dead; Victory songs
Wishram Indians
  Washington, Wishram

        Dance songs; Lodge songs
    Yakima Indians
      Washington, Yakima Indian Reservation
        Dance songs; Healing songs; Love songs; Medicine
        songs
  United States or Canada
    Acoma Indians
      Unknown locations
        Dance songs; Kachinas; Mask songs
    Arikara Indians
      Unknown locations
        Corn ceremonies; Medicine songs; Speeches,
        addresses, etc.
    [Arikara Indians]
      Unknown locations
        Medicine songs
    Hidatsa Indians
      Unknown locations
        Medicine songs
    Makah Indians
      Unknown locations
        Whaling songs
    Mandan Indians
      Unknown locations
        Turtle songs
    Paloos Indians
      Unknown locations
        Gambling songs
    Piegan Indians
      Unknown locations
        Dance songs; Lodge songs; Medicine bundle songs;
        Medicine songs; Mythology--Siksika; Rites and
        ceremonies; Scouts' songs; Society songs; War
        songs
    Tamonas Indians [?]
      Unknown locations
        Medicine songs
    Tewa Indians
      Unknown locations
        Snake dance songs
    Twadux Indians [?]
      Unknown locations
        Gambling songs; Ghost songs; Medicine songs;
        Speeches, addresses, etc.
    Unknown culture groups
      Union City
        Potlatch songs; Warriors' songs
      Unknown locations
        Love songs; Puberty rites (female); Puberty rites
        (male); Rejoicing songs

Number of cylinders: 279
Number of strips: 463
Sound quality of strips: EX 14, G 148, F 218, P 55,
        VP 11, B 12, U 5.
Degree of restriction: 1

   Indiana University purchased this collection in 1956
from the Charles Lauriat Company. Although large, this
collection is not complete. The remaining Curtis
cylinders, estimated at several thousand, are scattered
throughout the world; for the most part, their whereabouts
is not documented.
   Twenty-seven Indian groups are represented by this
particular collection. Of these groups, the Mandan,
Hidatsa, Piegan, Salish, Cheyenne, Shoshoni, and Kwakiutl
are the best represented. The documentation for the
Archives collection is inconsistent, showing little
information for the Mandan and Hidatsa material, and good
notes, including names of informants, for Shoshoni,
Arapaho, Kwakiutl recordings.
   Between the years 1907 and 1930, Curtis compiled a
twenty-volume work, The North American Indian, which
included selections from over forty thousand photographs
as well as information about games, myths, sacred rites,
and music of all of the Indian groups he had visited.
Five hundred sets of The North American Indian were
printed, and only 272 were bound. One of these sets is at
the Lilly Library of Indiana University.

59-002-F. Various collectors, Berlin Phonogramm-Archiv,
           1900-1913.
   Angola
     Ngangela (Bantu people)
       Mission Station Kasindi
         Unknown subjects
   Argentina
     Ona Indians
       Tierra del Fuego, Haberton, Beagle Channel
         Invectives and derisions; Medicine men's songs
   [Argentina and Chile]
     Toba Indians
       Patagonia Region
         Unknown subjects
   [Argentina, Bolivia, and Paraguay]
     Unknown culture groups
       Gran Chaco Region
         Unknown subjects
   Australia
     Australian Aborigines
       Western Australia, Beagle Bay Mission, Niolniol
         Unknown subjects
   Brazil
     Desana Indians
       Unknown locations
         Flute music
     Macusi Indians
       Rio Surumú
         Grinding songs
   Burma
     Burmese

      Mandalay Province
        Instrumental music; Stories, narratives and
        anecdotes
      Unknown locations
        Instrumental music
  Cameroon
    Bamum (African people)
      Unknown locations
        Flute music; Instrumental music; Unknown subjects
  Canada
    Assiniboin Indians
      [Alberta?]
        War songs
    Cree Indians
      Unknown locations
        War dance songs
    Ntlakyapamuk Indians
      British Columbia
        Game songs
  China
    Chinese
      Peking
        Flute music; Instrumental music; Theater music
      Szechuan, Yangtse River [District]
        Rowing songs
      Unknown locations
        Instrumental music; Unknown subjects
  Congo (Brazzaville)
    Bakongo (African people)
      Madzia Station
        Boys' songs; Dance songs
      Unknown locations
        Dance songs; Funeral rites and ceremonies;
        Healing songs; Laments[?]; Planting songs;
        Women's songs
  Equatorial Guinea
    Wapangwa (Bantu people)
      Bata Hinterland, Station Bebai
        Chants; Funeral rites and ceremonies
      Unknown locations
        Unknown subjects
  Ethiopia
    Unknown culture groups
      Unknown locations
        Soldiers' songs; War songs
  Germany, West [orig. of inf.: Cameroon]
    Bula (African people)
      Berlin, Phongramm-Archiv
        War songs
    Eton (African people)
      Berlin, Phongramm-Archiv
        Signals[?]; Signals (Drum)
  Germany, West [orig. of inf.: India]
    Muslims
      Berlin [orig. of inf.: Hyderabad]
        Instrumental music

    Germany, West [orig. of inf.: Japan]
      Japanese
        Berlin, Phonogramm-Archiv
          Instrumental music
    Germany, West [orig. of inf.: Soviet Union]
      Samoyeds
        Berlin, Nordland Exposition (1911: Berlin)
          Unknown subjects
    Germany, West [orig. of inf.: Sri Lanka]
      Sinhalese
        Berlin
          Dance songs
    Germany, West [orig. of inf.: Thailand]
      Thais
        Berlin, Phonogramm-Archiv
          Instrumental music
    Germany, West [orig. of inf.: United States]
      Hopi Indians
        Berlin
          Chants; Funeral rites and ceremonies
    Greenland
      Eskimos
        East Greenland
          Unknown subjects
    Guyana
      Arecuna Indians
        Unknown locations
          Healing songs; Medicine men's songs
      Macusi Indians
        Unknown locations
          Dance songs
    India
      Gujaratis (Indic people)
        Unknown locations
          Instrumental music
    Indonesia
      Unknown culture groups
        Sumatra
          Unknown subjects
      Alfures
        Moluccas, Ceram
          Dance songs
      Balinese (Indonesian people)
        Bali
          Instrumental music
      Engganese (Indonesian people)
        Unknown locations
          Funeral rites and ceremonies
      Javanese
        Java
          Instrumental music; Unknown subjects
      Unknown culture groups
        Borneo
          Instrumental music; Unknown subjects
        Borneo, Oedjoe Halang
          Unknown subjects

        Celebes
          Unknown subjects
        Sumatra
          Flute music; Love songs
        Sumatra, Fort de Kock
          Instrumental music
  Israel
    Sephardim
      Jerusalem
        Sacred songs
  Japan
    Japanese
      Unknown locations
        Instrumental music; Men's songs
  Mexico
    Huichol Indians
      Unknown locations
        Agricultural songs
      Rancho Los Cancos
        Corn songs
    Unknown culture groups
      Unknown locations
        Unknown subjects
  Micronesia (Federated States)
    Unknown culture groups
      Caroline Islands, Ponape
        Unknown subjects
      Caroline Islands, Truk Island
        Love songs
  Papau New Guinea
    Kiwai (Papuan people)
      Unknown locations
        Funeral rites and ceremonies
    Unknown culture groups
      Admiralty Islands
        Dance songs; Drum music[?]
      Bougainville Island, [Solomon Islands]
        Unknown subjects
      Bougainville Island, Telei [Solomon Islands]
        Unknown subjects
      Dampier Island
        Lullabies; Speeches, addresses, etc.
      Green Islands, Nissan
        Laments
      Huon Gulf
        Love songs
      New Britain Island, Gazelle Peninsula
        Unknown subjects
      New Britain Island, Gazelle Half-Island,
      Herbertshöhe
        Women's dance songs
      New Ireland Island
        Women's dance songs
      Seleo at Berlin Harbor
        Unknown subjects
      Valis Island at Berlin Harbor

         Unknown subjects
Somalia
  Unknown culture groups
    Unknown locations
      Instrumental music
South Africa
  Unknown culture groups
    Johannesburg
      Unknown subjects
Soviet Union
  Byelorussians
    Unknown locations
      Instrumental music
  Oroches
    Unknown locations
      Shamans' songs
  Permians
    Komi Autonomous Republic [or South Russia],
    Sintamovy
      Girls' songs; Invectives and derisions; Spring
      songs
  Tatars
    Unknown locations
      Love songs; Stories, narratives and anecdotes;
      Unknown subjects
Sri Lanka
  Veddahs
    Bibile
      Unknown subjects
Sudan
  Baguirmi (African people)
    Unknown locations
      Unknown subjects
Switzerland
  Swiss
    Unknown locations
      Unknown subjects
[Tanzania]
  Chaga (African people)
    Unknown locations
      Unknown subjects
  Haya (African people)
    Unknown locations
      Instrumental music
  Luvemba (African people)[?]
    Mzobi
      Unknown subjects
  Masai
    Arusha
      Chants; War songs
  Nyamwezi
    Unknown locations
      Drinking songs
  Sandawe
    Unknown locations
      Dance songs

        Unknown culture groups
          Unknown locations
            Women's dance songs
        Wazaramo (African people)
          Unknown locations
            Dance songs
        Zigula (Bantu people)
          Unknown locations
            Instrumental music
        Zinza (African people)
          Unknown locations
            Unknown subjects
  [Tanzania?]
      Babwende (Bantu people)[?]
        Unknown locations
          Women's dance songs
      Manyemen (African people)[?]
        Unknown locations
          Women's dance songs
      Valuga (African people)[?]
        Unknown locations
          Children's songs
      Waitaku (African people)[?]
        Unknown locations
          Unknown subjects
  Togo
    Ewe (African people)
      Unknown locations
        Laments[?]
    Hausas
      Unknown locations
        Drum music; Instrumental music; Signals (drum)[?]
    Unknown subjects
      Unknown locations
        Instrumental music; Unknown subjects
  Tunisia
    Berbers (Moroccan)
      Unknown locations
        Unknown subjects
    Tunisians
      Tunis
        Dance music; Flute music
      Unknown locations
        Dance music; Unknown subjects
  United States
    Pawnee Indians
      Oklahoma
        Ghost dance songs
  Western Samoa
    Samoans[?]
      Savai'i Island [Sawaii]
        Farewell songs
  Zaire
    Ruandas (African people)
      Mulera Land, Ruasa
        Chants; Festival songs

Number of cylinders: 120
Number of strips: 149
Sound quality of strips: EX 12, G 68, F 58, P 7, U 4.
Degree of restriction: 1

The Demonstration Collection of the Berlin Phonogramm-
Archiv represents the first anthology of traditional music
ever issued. The recordings were selected and the sets
distributed by Erich M. von Hornbostel. In 1931, he used
one set of the collection for teaching "Music of the
World's Peoples," at the New School for Social Research,
in New York City. The collection has figured strongly in
the development of the discipline of ethnomusicology.

This set of recordings was deposited at the Archives by
the New School for Social Research. The cylinders are
first generation copies of von Hornbostel's original
recordings. Forty-two cylinders from this collection and
from George Herzog's set of the Demonstration Collection
were reproduced in 1963 for a two disc album entitled "The
Demonstration Collection of E.M. von Hornbostel and the
Berlin Phonogramm-Archiv," produced by the Indiana
University Archives of Folk and Primitive Music
Ethnomusicological Series, and edited by George List and
Kurt Reinhard (Ethnic Folkways Library FE 4175). The
recordings used for this publication are very well
documented, often with musical transcriptions.

Of the 116 cylinders recorded by the Cylinder Project,
only seven are of poor sound quality. Many of the
recordings are of good fidelity and are therefore of
inestimable value, considering their history, the extent
and accuracy of their documentation and their broad
geographic distribution.

Reference:
List, George. "A Secular Sermon for Those of the
Ethnomusicological Faith," _Ethnomusicology_, Vol 27, No. 2
(May 1983), pp. 175-186.
Folkways discs: see collection 65-038-C.

Related collection: 83-899-F

60-004-F. Leslie A. White, 1927-1928.
    United States
      Acoma Indians
        New Mexico, Acomita
          Corn dance songs; Kachinas
        Unknown locations
          Corn dance songs; Eagle dance songs; Unknown
          subjects
      Acoma Indians (inf.); Comanche Indians (item)
        New Mexico, Acomita
          Dance songs
        Unknown locations
          Dance songs

        Keresan Indians
          New Mexico, Santo Domingo
            Kachinas
        Navaho Indians
          New Mexico, Santo Domingo
            Corn dance songs; Dance songs; Kachinas; Unknown
            subjects

Number of cylinders: 10
Number of strips: 14
Sound quality of strips: G 11, F 2, P 1.
Degree of restriction: 1

   Documentation for this collection was taken from
inscriptions on the cylinder boxes and from correspondence
from the collector. Dates, place names, and descriptions
of the songs are available in most cases, but informants'
names are not generally mentioned.
   Leslie White and George Herzog collaborated in making
the 1927 Acoma recordings in this collections. The
remainder of the cylinders may be found under accession
number 54-101-F. Additional Acoma recordings that White
made during the summer of 1927 were deposited in the
Grosvenor Library in Buffalo, New York.

60-017-F. Edward Sapir, 1910.
    United States
      Cheyenne Indians
        Unknown locations
          Peyote songs
      Hopi Indians
        Unknown locations
          Buffalo dance songs; Buffalo songs; Butterfly
          dance songs; Coyote dance songs; Coyote songs;
          Kachinas; Rabbit songs; Unknown subjects; War
          dance songs; Women's dance songs; Women's songs
      Kickapoo Indians
        Unknown locations
          Peyote songs
      Oto Indians
        Unknown locations
          Unknown subjects
      Paiute Indians
        Pennsylvania, Philadelphia
          Bear dance songs; Coyote songs; Dance songs;
          Gambling songs; Ghost dance songs; Greeting
          songs; Hunting songs; Laments; Medicine men's
          songs; Mythology; Rites and ceremonies; Round
          dance songs; Scalp dance songs; Unknown subjects;
          War songs
      Paiute Indians (inf.); Shoshoni Indians (item)
        Unknown locations
          Laments; Round dance songs
      Paiute Indians (inf.); Hualapai Indians (item)
        Unknown locations

       Ghost dance songs
    Paiute Indians (inf.); Ute Indians (item)
      Unknown locations
        Dance songs
    Shawnee Indians
      Unknown locations
        Dance songs; Women's songs

Number of cylinders: 128
Number of strips: 131
Sound quality of strips: F 17, P 32, VP 79, B 3.
Degree of restriction: 2

    This large collection was received for deposit from the
University Museum, University of Pennsylvania, in 1960.
The Paiute section of the collection is very well
documented, but little information is available for the
remainder of the recordings. The Archives holds
transcriptions made by Jacob Sapir for the Paiute
cylinders. It is very fortunate that these transcriptions
were made since most of the cylinders are now of poor or
very poor sound quality.
    Tony Tillohash, a southern Paiute from Kanab, Utah, was
the single performer for all the Paiute items.

60-018-F. Frank Gouldsmith Speck, ca. 1905-1911.
    United States or Canada
      Abnaki Indians
        Unknown locations
          Dance songs
      Algonquian Indians
        Unknown locations
          Unknown subjects
      French-Canadians and Montagnais Indians
        Unknown locations
          Unknown subjects
      Huron Indians
        Unknown locations
          Chants; Hymns; Marriage rites and ceremonies; War
          dance songs
      Malecite Indians
        Unknown locations
          Children's songs; Greeting songs; Humorous songs;
          Hymns; Love songs; Mythology; Unknown subjects;
          War dance songs
      Malecite Indians (item); Penobscot Indians (item)
        Unknown locations
          Unknown subjects
      Micmac Indians
        Unknown locations
          Dance songs; Drinking songs; Love songs; Unknown
          subjects; War dance songs
      Micmac Indians[?]
        Unknown locations

        Love songs
    Micmac Indians and Malecite Indians
       Unknown locations
        Love songs
    Micmac Indians and Beothuk Indians
       Unknown locations
        Unknown subjects
    Montagnais Indians
       Unknown locations
        Lullabies; Unknown subjects
    Montagnais Indians[?] (inf.); French-Canadians (item)
       Unknown locations
        Unknown subjects
    Pamunkey Indians
       Unknown locations
        Lullabies
    Penobscot Indians
       Unknown locations
        Dance songs; Death songs; Drinking songs;
        Greeting songs; Humorous songs; Love songs;
        Lullabies; Marriage rites and ceremonies; Snake
        dance songs; Unknown subjects; War dance songs
    Penobscot Indians[?]
       Unknown locations
        Unknown subjects
    Penobscot Indians (item); Malecite Indians (item)
       Unknown locations
        Dance songs
    Penobscot Indians (item); Micmac Indians (item)
       Unknown locations
        Dance songs
    Unknown culture groups
       Unknown locations
        Dance songs; Marriage rites and ceremonies; Snake
        dance songs; Unknown subjects; War dance songs

Number of cylinders: 79
Number of strips: 120
Sound quality of strips: F 46,   P 47,   VP 26,   B 1.
Degree of restriction: 2

    The documentation for this collection is inconsistent.
At times, only the name of the culture group is given for
a particular item. Other cylinder recordings are
accompanied by the culture group name, the name of the
informant, the location of the recording, the date, and
the title.
    Further information about Dr. Speck's research may be
acquired by investigating the following:
  Speck, Frank G. Penobscot Man, the Life History of a
Forest Tribe in Maine (1940).
    Cassell, Nancy A. "American Ethnologist Frank Gouldsmith
Speck," Resound, Vol. II, No. 1., Jan., 1983.

60-019-F. Collector Unknown, ca. 1910.
    Nigeria
      Fon (African people)
        Unknown locations
          Unknown subjects
      Yorubas
        Unknown locations
          Dance songs; Death songs; Drum music; Hunting
          songs[?]; Love songs; Lullabies; Prayers;
          Speeches, addresses, etc.; Spring songs; Stories,
          narratives and anecdotes; Unknown subjects; War
          dance songs; War songs

Number of cylinders: 20
Number of strips: 24
Sound quality of strips: EX 1, G 14, F 9.
Degree of restriction: 2

   This is an incomplete collection deposited in the
Archives by the University Museum of the University of
Pennsylvania. The documentation, gathered from original
cylinder box inscriptions, varies in content. One
informant, Hambopolo, is identified for three cylinders
only.
   One of the recordings of African drumming, SCY 5135, is
of excellent quality.

60-026-F. Séamus O'Duilearga, ca. 1930.
    Ireland
      Irish
        Ballycroy, An Cloigeaun
          Stories, narratives and anecdotes

Number of cylinders: 1
Number of strips: 1
Sound quality of strips: G 1.
Degree of restriction: 1

   This one large cylinder was given to the Archives of
Traditional Music by the late Stith Thompson. It is not
clear whether O'Duilearga made this recording or whether
he simply brought the cylinder to Indiana University,
where it became the property of Stith Thompson.
   The location of the recording is An Cloigeavn,
Ballycroy. The informant, Paohraic MacMeanman recites a
folktale in Irish Gaelic. Frank Wright, a Gaelic linguist
at Indiana University, assisted in documenting this
recording.

63-042-F. Samuel Alfred Barrett, 1911.
    United States
      Hopi Indians
        [Arizona]
          Unknown subjects

Number of cylinders: 17
Number of strips: 29
Sound quality of strips: EX 3,   G 15,   F 10,   P 1.
Degree of restriction: 1

   This collection of cylinders, from an original group of
98, was donated to the Archives of Traditional Music by
the Milwaukee Public Museum. Barrett's typescript
manuscript, "Notes on Hopi Songs Recorded by S.A. Barrett
in 1911 for the Milwaukee Public Museum," provides
complete documentation for the Archives' collection and
the remainder of the cylinders, which were deposited at
the Library of Congress.

64-040-F. James Willard Schultz, ca. 1926.
     Canada
       Siksika Indians
         Unknown locations
           Dance songs; Rabbit dance songs
       Siksika Indians (item)
         Unknown locations
           Dance songs; Love songs; Owl dance songs; Victory
           songs; War dance songs[?]

Number of cylinders: 5
Number of strips: 5
Sound quality of strips: F 4,   P 1.
Degree of restriction: 1

   In 1964 Mrs. Jesse Schultz, widow of James W. Schultz,
deposited these cylinders in the Archives through Carling
Malouf at Montana State University. Mr. Schultz had lived
some fifty years with the Siksika.
   Documentation for this collection was compiled from
announcements on the recordings and from notes prepared by
Naomi Ware, Archives assistant at the time the collection
was received. Ware combined information on slips of paper
found inside the cylinder boxes, inscriptions on the boxes
themselves, and a list of audible announcements on the
cylinders.
   The performers include Frank and Rose Gardner, Frank
Stewart, Jack Stewart, and Isaac P. Hoops.

References:
Schultz, James Willard. My Life as an Indian. New York,
1935.

_____. Blackfeet and Buffalo. Norman:
University of Oklahoma Press, 1962.

67-151-F. Melville Jean and Francis Shapiro Herskovits,
           1928-1929.
    Haiti
      Haitians
        Port-au-Prince
          Sacred songs
      Haitians (item)
        Port-au-Prince
          Sacred songs
    Surinam
      Djuka (Surinam people)
        Kofi Kamp
          Dance songs; Sacred songs; Unknown subjects
        Paramaribo
          Dance songs; Fertility dance songs; Invectives
          and derisions; Sacred songs; Snake songs; Social
          dance songs; Stories, narratives and anecdotes;
          Unknown subjects
      Saramacca (Surinam people)
        Unknown locations
          Celebrations; Cult songs; Dance songs; Funeral
          rites and ceremonies; Greeting songs; Prayers;
          Sacred songs; Snake songs; Songs of thanks;
          Spirit songs; Stories, narratives and anecdotes;
          Unknown subjects; Work songs

Number of cylinders: 100
Number of strips: 396
Sound quality of strips: F 249, P 100, VP 32, B 14,
        U 1.
Degree of restriction: 1

    This is a complete set of cylinders recorded by Melville
J. Herskovits and his wife, Frances, during the summers of
1928 and 1929. The purpose of these expeditions was to
study the cultural life of blacks from the coastal city of
Paramaribo, and the "Bush Negro" tribes, the Saramacca and
the Djuka, from the more isolated inland areas.   This
collection contains a variety of religious, secular and
ancestral cult songs, most of which were transcribed by
ethnomusicologist Mieczslaw Kolinski in the publication
which resulted from the expeditions: Herskovits, Melville
J. and Frances S. Suriname Folk-Lore. New York: Columbia
University Press, 1936.
    It is unfortunate, with such impressive documentation,
that the sound quality of these cylinders is consistently
poor. Most of the recordings are marred by surface noise,
due to film leaching and spots of mold on the cylinder
surface and by machine noise, a hum acquired during the
original "cutting" of the cylinders on an Edison machine.

67-152-F. Melville Jean and Frances Shapiro Herskovits,
           1931.
    Ghana
      Ashantis (African people)

Asokore
  Children's songs[?]; Dance songs; Funeral rites
  and ceremonies; Hunting songs; Laments; Love
  songs; Puberty rites (female); Snake songs; Songs
  of honor and praise; Unknown subjects; Women's
  dance songs; Women's songs; Work songs
Nigeria
  Fon (African people)
    Abomey
      Chants; Children's songs; Cult songs; Dance
      songs; Funeral rites and ceremonies; Hunting
      songs; Invectives and derisions; Lullabies;
      Marriage rites and ceremonies; Personal songs;
      Prayers; Puberty rites, (female)[?]; Rites and
      ceremonies; Society songs[?]; Songs for the dead;
      Songs of allusion; Songs of honor and praise;
      Songs of thanks; Speeches, addresses, etc.;
      Stories, narratives and anecdotes, (songs from);
      Unknown subjects; Warriors' songs; Women's songs;
      Work songs
    Allada
      Agricultural songs; Chiefs' songs[?]; Cult songs;
      Dance songs; Flute music; Grinding songs; Hunting
      songs; Instrumental music; Invectives and
      derisions; Marriage rites and ceremonies; Rites
      and ceremonies; Songs of allusion; Songs of
      thanks; Stories, narratives and anecdotes (songs
      from); Unknown subjects; Women's songs; Work
      songs
    Whydah
      Songs of allusion; Unknown subjects; Work songs
  Mina (Africa people)
    Abomey
      Proverb songs; Songs of honor and praise
  Sobo (African people)
    Lagos
      Spirit songs; Unknown subjects
  Yorubas
    Abeoluta
      Stories, narratives and anecdotes (songs from);
      Unknown subjects
    Ibadan
      Unknown subjects
    Unknown locations
      Proverb songs; Unknown subjects
[Nigeria]
  Unknown culture groups
    Unknown locations
      Unknown subjects
  Yorubas
    Unknown locations
      Unknown subjects

Number of cylinders: 242
Number of strips: 657
Sound quality of strips: F 457, P 114, VP 71, B 14,

NR 1.
Degree of restriction: 1

   This is a very large but apparently incomplete
collection of cylinders collected by Melville J.
Herskovits and his wife and co-author, Frances S.
Herskovits. Mrs. Herskovits donated this collection to
the Archives in 1963.

69-015-F/C. Frederick A. Starr, 1906.
   Zaire
      Bangi (African people)
         Bolobo
            Instrumental music
      Luba (African people)
         Lower Kasai District, Ndombe
            Bawdy songs; Instrumental music; Unknown subjects
      Luba and Kuba (African peoples)
         Lower Kasai District, Ndombe
            Instrumental music
      Unknown culture groups
         Lake Tumba, Ikoko
            Instrumental music
         Lower Kasai District, Ndombe
            Instrumental music
   [Zaire]
      Unknown culture groups
         Unknown locations
            Unknown subjects

Number of cylinders: 68
Number of strips: 68
Sound quality of strips: EX 2, G 28, F 26, P 10, U 2.
Degree of restriction: 1

   Of these 68 cylinders, 16 are original field recordings,
and the rest are Columbia "indestructible cylinder"
copies. They were donated to the Archives by Patricia and
Ralph Altman.
   The collector was a well-known biologist, ethnologist,
geographer, geologist, and anthropologist, who worked at
the American Museum of Natural History, Pomona College,
and the University of Chicago. His field expeditions took
him to Mexico, Guatemala, the Congo, Japan, Korea, the
Philippines, Cuba, and Liberia.
   In a valuable article on the Starr Congo recordings,
Frank J. Gillis gives the history of the expedition,
including excerpts from Starr's field notebooks. These
notebooks, now in the Department of Special Collections at
the University of Chicago, give descriptions of the
contents of the cylinder recordings, and often include
valuable ethnomusicological interpretations.
   Many of the performances in this collection feature
instruments such as the musical bow, the ocarina, the
notched rattle, and a variety of whistles. The vocal

selections are mainly of group songs. Even if a solo
performer is featured, he is accompanied by a male chorus.

Reference:
Gillis, Frank J. "The Starr Collection of Recordings from
the Congo (1906) in the Archives of Traditional Music."
The Folklore and Folk Music Archivist, Vol. X, No. 3,
Spring 1968, pp. 49-62.

75-199-C. Frederick A. Starr, ca. 1910-1912.
   United States
      Americans
         Columbia Recording Labs
            Dance songs; Folk-songs; Instrumental music;
            Jigs; Marches; Music, Popular; Waltzes
      Americans (inf.); Germans (item)
         Columbia Recording Labs
            Music, Popular; Operas--Excerpts

Number of cylinders: 16
Number of strips: 16
Sound quality of strips: EX 16.
Degree of restriction: 1

   This collection of commercial cylinders from the estate
of Frederick A. Starr was donated by Ralph C. Altman to
the Archives of Traditional Music in 1962. The selections
recorded are typical popular vocal and instrumental songs
of the beginning of the centruy. Included are
"Introduction to the Third Act of Lohengrin," "The Father
of Victory, March, " "Street Piano Medley," "Estellita
Waltz," and others.

80-084-C. Frank J. Gillis, donor, ca. 1910-1925.
   United States
      Americans
         Edison Recording Labs
            Dance music; Music, Popular
         Unknown locations
            Dance song; Folk-songs; Music, Popular; Waltzes

Number of cylinders: 25
Number of strips: 25
Sound quality of strips: EX 10 , G 9, F 6.
Degree of restriction: 1

   Fifteen of these cylinders are Edison commercial
recordings; the others are of uncertain origin. The
documentation has been complied from the etched
inscriptions on the rim of each cylinder, and from
occasional cylinder announcements.
   The selections performed offer a wide variety of popular
musics, such as "Turkey in the Straw," "Alexander's
Ragtime Band," "Temptation Rag," "The Blacksmith Rag,"

several barn dances, and many others. A few coon songs
are also included.

80-085-C. John Edward Hasse, donor, ca. 1910-1925.
   United States
      Americans
         Columbia Recording Labs
            Music, Popular
         Edison Recording Labs
            Music, Popular

Number of cylinders: 4
Number of strips: 4
Sound quality of strips: G 1, F 1, P 1, VP 1.
Degree of restriction: 1

   These four cylinders contain two coon songs, one banjo
solo, and a popular song of the period, "Red Wing."
Documentation was compiled from information etched on the
cylinder rims and from aural announcements on the
recordings themselves.

80-086-C. Unknown depositor, ca. 1910-1925.
   United States
      Americans
         Edison Recording Labs
            Ballets--Excerpts; Music, Popular; Operas--
            Excerpts; Waltzes
         Unknown locations
            Unknown subjects

Number of cylinders: 7
Number of strips: 7
Sound quality of strips: EX 2, G 2, P 1, B 2.
Degree of restriction: 1

   The chief performer of these commercial cylinders is the
Edison Military Band. The selections include "Swedish
March," "American Student [?] Waltz," and others. Another
recording is a solo from Mozart's "The Magic Flute,"
played on a set of bells. Documentation has come from the
cylinder inscriptions and from announcements.

83-889-C. Herbert Halpert, donor, ca. 1910-1925.
   United States
      Americans
         Columbia Recording Labs
            Instrumental music; Music, Popular; Polkas
         Edison Recording Labs
            Marches; Music, Popular; Patriotic music; Sacred
            songs; Vaudeville
      Italians
         Edison Recording Labs

Opera--Excerpts

Number of cylinders: 25
Number of strips: 25
Sound quality of strips: G 14,   F 8,   P 1,   VP 2.
Degree of restriction: 1

Documentation for this large collection of commercial
cylinders was compiled from etchings on the rims of the
cylinders containing song titles and matrix numbers.

83-890-F. Herbert Halpert, ca. 1930.
    United States
      Americans
        New Jersey
          Folk-songs; Unknown subjects

Number of cylinders: 3
Number of strips: 3
Sound quality of strips: VP 3.
Degree of restriction: 3

This is most likely an incomplete collection, as it
contains only three field recorded cylinders from New
Jersey, possibly the Pine Barrens, where Halpert did much
of his folklore and folk music research.
As these cylinders lacked written documentation, the
only information available was that which could be heard
on the recordings themselves. This task was made almost
impossible by the very poor sound quality of the
cylinders. The first cylinder many contain an Anglo-
American song, "Down in the Valley." The other two
cylinders are incomprehensible, due to extreme surface
noise.

83-891-F. Richard Thurnwald, [1933?].
    Melanesia
      Unknown culture groups
        Unknown locations
          Unknown subjects

Number of cylinders: 29
Number of strips: 30
Sound quality of strips: VP 27,   B 3.
Degree of restriction: 1

This is apparently a complete collection.
Unfortunately, there is no documentation; the original
cylinder boxes contain numbers only, and the cylinders
contain no spoken announcements. The sound quality of all
twenty-nine cylinders is extremely poor; in most cases,
they are nearly inaudible. In short, there is practically
nothing of redeemable research value in these materials.

83-892-F. Manuel José Andrade, 1928.
    United States
        Quileute Indians
            Unknown locations
                Vocabulary and pronunciation[?]

Number of cylinders: 9
Number of strips: 12
Sound quality of strips: G 1, F 5, VP 6.
Degree of restriction: 2

    This small group of cylinders is not a complete
collection. One stray cylinder, obviously a part of the
Andrade materials, was found at the end of the Cylinder
Project, thousands of numbers away from its companions.
    There is a pertinent publication associated with this
collection, written by the collector: Andrade, Manuel
José. "Quileute Texts" in Columbia University
Contributions to Anthropology, Vol. 12. New York: Columbia
University Press, 1931.
    Specific documentation of each cylinder, however, is
virtually nonexistent. All nine recordings are speech,
possibly language training cylinders for the Quileute
dialect. Each section of speech is announced with a
number, spoken in English; some of the cylinders contain
as many as twenty sections.

83-893-F. Unknown collector, no date.
    United States
        Indians of North America (unidentified)
            Pacific Northwest Coast
                Lullabies; Unknown subjects; Speeches, addresses,
                etc.

Number of cylinders: 40
Number of strips: 42
Sound quality of strips: G 10, F 16, P 14, VP 1, B 1.
Degree of restriction: 2

    Little information is available for this collection.
The collector's numbers are consecutive. Some of the
original cylinder boxes contain the inscriptions
"Northwest Coast," which does give a clue as to the
location.
    Some cylinders contain group singing, although most are
solo unaccompanied male or female voices.

83-895-F. George Herzog, 1927[?].
    United States
        San Juan Indians
            New Mexico, San Juan Pueblo
                Unknown subjects

Number of cylinders: 2

Number of strips: 2
Sound quality of strips: G 2.
Degree of restriction: 2

   Documentation for these cylinders compiled from George
Herzog's inscriptions on the cylinder boxes is quite
sparse. The genres, song descriptions, and performers'
names are unknown.

83-896-F.   Louis Shotridge [?], ca. 1910.
    United States
      Athapascan Indians
       [Alaska]
          Unknown subjects
       Tlingit Indians[?]
          Unknown locations
             Dance songs; Laments; Rites and ceremonies;
             Unknown subjects
       Tsimshian Indians
          Unknown locations
             Unknown subjects
       Unknown culture groups
          Unknown locations
             Greeting songs

Number of cylinders: 8
Number of strips: 9
Sound quality of strips: F 2,   P 5,   VP 2.
Degree of restriction: 2

   This collection was recorded in 1960 at the University
Museum of the University of Pennsylvania. Correspondence
from J. Alden Mason to George Herzog in 1932 indicates
that the collector of these recordings was most likely
Louis Shotridge, a Tlingit Indian employed by the
University Museum in the 1900s.
   Documentation for these cylinders is sparse. The
culture group designations are uncertain, the informants
are not named, and the titles of the songs are
infrequently noted. Information has come from
inscriptions on the original cylinder boxes. The
handwriting on the boxes is the same as that of collection
60-017-F.

83-897-F.   Unknown collector, 1905-1911.
    United States
      Dakota Indians
        South Dakota, Pine Ridge
          Unknown subjects
      Unknown countries
        Unknown culture groups
          Unknown locations
            Unknown subjects

Number of cylinders: 10
Number of strips: 10
Sound quality of strips: P 5, VP 5.
Degree of restriction: 2

   There cylinders were received from the University
Museum, University of Pennsylvania, along with the Sapir
and Speck collections. They have virtually no
documentation. The only information regarding their
identification has been found on a note, attached to the
original cylinder boxes 5038 and 5045: "Unidentifed
cylinders are possibly from Sapir collection."

83-898-F. Unknown collector, no date.
   Unknown countries
      Unknown culture groups
         Unknown locations
            Unknown subjects

Number of cylinders: 2
Number of strips: 2
Sound quality of strips: P 1, VP 1.
Degree of restriction:

   These two cylinders have absolutely no accompanying
documentation. They are further removed from the
possibility of identification by the fact that both are of
poor sound quality.

83-899-F. Various collectors, Berlin Phonogramm-Archiv,
           1900-1913.
   Angola
      Ngangela (Bantu people)
         Mission Station Kasindi
            Unknown subjects
   Argentina
      Ona Indians
         Tierra del Fuego, Haberton, Beagle Channel
            Invectives and derisions; Medicine men's songs
   [Argentina, Bolivia, and Paraguay]
      Toba Indians
         Gran Chaco Region
            Unknown subjects
   [Argentina and Chile]
      Toba Indians
         Patagonia
            Unknown subjects
   Australia
      Australian Aborigines
         Western Australia, Beagle Bay Mission, Niolniol
            Unknown subjects
   Brazil
      Desana Indians
         Unknown locations

      Flute music
   Macusi Indians
     Rio Surumú
      Grinding songs
Burma
  Burmese
    Mandalay Province
     Stories, narratives and ancedotes
Cameroon
  Bamum (African people)
    Unknown locations
     Flute music; Instrumental music; Unknown subjects
Canada
  Assiniboin Indians
    [Alberta?]
     War songs
  Cree Indians
    Unknown locations
     War dance songs
  Ntlakyapamuk Indians
    British Columbia
     Game songs
China
  Chinese
    Peking
     Flute music; Instrumental music; Theater music
    Szechuan, Yangtse River [District]
     Rowing songs
    Unknown locations
     Instrumental music; Unknown subjects
Congo (Brazzaville)
  Bakongo (African people)
    Madzia Station
     Boys' songs; Dance songs
    Unknown locations
     Dance songs; Funeral rites and ceremonies;
     Healing songs; Laments; Planting songs; Women's
     songs
Equatorial Guinea
  Wapangwa (Bantu people)
    Bata Hinterland, Station Bebai
     Chants; Funeral rites and ceremonies
    Unknown locations
    Unknown subjects
Ethiopia
  Unknown culture groups
    Unknown locations
     Soldiers' songs; War songs
Germany, West [orig. of inf.: Cameroon]
  Bula (African people)
    Berlin, Phonogramm-Archiv
     War songs
  Eton (African people)
    Berlin, Phonogramm-Archiv
     Signals[?]; Signals (Drum)
Germany, West [orig. of inf.: India]

    Muslims[?]
      Berlin [orig. of inf.: Hyderabad]
        Instrumental music
  Germany, West [orig. of inf.: Japan]
    Japanese
      Berlin, Phonogramm-Archiv
        Instrumental music
  Germany, West [orig. of inf.: Somoan Islands?]
    Samoans[?]
      Berlin, Phonogramm-Archiv
        Unknown subjects
  Germany, West [orig. of inf.: Soviet Union]
    Samoyeds
      Berlin, Nordland Exposition (1911: Berlin)
        Unknown subjects
  Germany, West [orig. of inf.: Sri Lanka]
    Sinhalese
      Berlin
        Dance songs
  Germany, West [orig. of inf.: United States]
    Hopi Indians
      Berlin
        Chants; Funeral rites and ceremonies
  Greenland
    Eskimos
      East Greenland
        Unknown subjects
  Guyana
    Arecuna Indians
      Unknown locations
        Healing songs; Medicine men's songs
    Macusi Indians
      Unknown locations
        Dance songs
  India
    [Gurkhas?]
      Unknown locations
        Unknown subjects
  Indonesia
    Alfures
      Moluccas, Ceram
        Dance songs
    Balinese (Indonesian people) [?]
      Bali
        Instrumental music
    Engganese (Indonesian people) [?]
      Unknown locations
        Funeral rites and ceremonies
    Unknown culture groups
      Borneo
        Instrumental music; Unknown subjects
      Borneo, Oedjoe Halang
        Unknown subjects
      Celebes
        Unknown subjects
      Sumatra

       Flute music; Love songs; Unknown subjects
     Sumatra, Fort de Kock
       Instrumental music
Japan
  Japanese
    Unknown locations
      Instrumental music
Korea
  Koreans
    Unknown locations
      Folk-songs
[Malawi]
  Angoni
    Unknown locations
      Unknown subjects
[Malawi?]
  Nyanja (African people)
    Unknown locations
      Unknown subjects
Malaysia
  Unknown culture groups
    Malay Peninsula
      Unknown subjects
Mexico
  Huichol Indians
    Ranchos Los Cancos
      Corn songs
  Unknown culture groups
    Unknown locations
      Unknown subjects
Micronesia (Federated States)
  Unknown culture groups
    Caroline Islands, Ponape
      Unknown subjects
    Caroline Islands, Truk Island
      Love songs
Mozambique
  Vandau (Bantu people)
    Unknown locations
      Unknown subjects
Papau New Guinea
  Kiwai (Papuan people)
    Unknown locations
      Funeral rites and ceremonies
  Unknown culture groups
    Admiralty Islands
      Dance songs; Drum music
    Bougainville Island, [Solomon Islands]
      Unknown subjects
    Bougainville Island, Telei [Solomon Islands]
      Unknown subjects
    Dampier Island
      Lullabies; Speeches, addresses, etc.
    Green Islands, Nissan
      Laments
    Huon Gulf

         Love songs
      New Britain Island, Gazelle Peninsula
         Unknown subjects
      New Britain Island, Gazelle Half-Island,
      Herbertshöhe
         Women's dance songs
      New Ireland Island
         Women's dance songs
      Seleo at Berlin Harbor
         Unknown subjects
      Valis Island at Berlin Harbor
         Unknown subjects
Somalia
   Unknown culture groups
      Unknown locations
         Instrumental music
South Africa
   Unknown culture groups
      Johannesburg
         Unknown subjects
Soviet Union
   Byelorussians
      Unknown locations
         Instrumental music
   Oroches[?]
      Unknown locations
         Shamans' songs
   Permians
      Komi Autonomous Republic [or South Russia],
      Sintamovy
         Girl's songs; Invectives and derisions; Spring
         songs
   Tatars
      Unknown locations
         Love songs; Stories, narratives and anecdotes;
         Unknown subjects
[Soviet Union?]
   Chuvashes
      [Chuvash Autonomous Republic?]
         Unknown subjects
   Chuvashes [?]
      Unknown locations
         Unknown subjects
   Georgians (Transcaucasians)
      Unknown locations
         Unknown subjects
   Unknown culture groups
      Unknown locations
         Instrumental music[?]
Sri Lanka
   Veddahs
      Bibile
         Unknown subjects
Sudan
   Baguirmi (African people)
      Unknown locations

          Unknown subjects
    Switzerland
      Swiss
        Unknown locations
          Unknown subjects
    Tanzania
      Masai
        Arusha
          Chants; War songs
    [Tanzania]
      Chaga (African people)
        Unknown locations
          Unknown subjects
      Haya (African people)
        Unknown locations
          Instrumental music
      Luvemba (African people)[?]
        Mzobi [East Africa]
          Unknown subjects
      Nyamwezi
        Unknown locations
          Drinking songs
      Sandawe
        Unknown locations
          Dance songs
      Unknown culture groups
        Unknown locations
          Women's dance songs
      Wamwera (African people)
        Unknown locations
          Instrumental music
      Wazaramo (African people)
        Unknown locations
          Dance songs
      Zigula (Bantu people)
        Unknown locations
          Instrumental music
      Zinza (African people)
        Unknown locations
          Unknown subjects
    [Tanzania?]
      Babwende (Bantu people)[?]
        Unknown locations
          Women's dance songs
      Manyemen (African people)[?]
        Unknown locations
          Women's dance songs
      Valuga (African people)[?]
        Unknown locations
          Children's songs
      Waitaku (African people)[?]
        Unknown locations
          Unknown subjects
    Togo
      Ewe (African people)
        Unknown locations

           Laments[?]
       Hausas
         Unknown locations
           Instrumental music
       Unknown culture groups
         Unknown locations
           Drum music; Instrumental music; Signals
           (Drum)[?]; Unknown subjects
     Unknown countries
       Chinese
         Unknown locations
           Unknown subjects
       Unknown culture groups
         Unknown locations
           Unknown subjects
     Western Samoa
       Samoans
         Savai'i Island [Sawaii]
           Farewell songs
     Zaire
       Ruandas (African people)
         Mulera Land, Ruasa
           Chants; Festival songs

Number of cylinders: 120
Number of strips: 153
Sound quality of strips: G 74, F 70, P 7.
Degree of restriction: 1

   This is a complete set of galvanoplastic cylinder copies
of the Berlin Phonogramm-Archiv Demonstration Collection
acquired from the estate of Dr. George Herzog. At least
twenty of the items in this collection are different from
the earlier collection, 59-002-F (Berlin Phonogramm-Archiv
Demonstration Collection), which was deposited at Indiana
University in 1961 by Henry Cowell of the New School for
Social Research, New York, NY. Documentation for these 20
items is sparse.
   The researcher will benefit from consulting the earlier
collection copies (59-002-F) as well as tape copies of the
related Folkways discs, "The Demonstration Collection of
E.M. von Hornbostel and the Berlin Phonogramm-Archiv"
(65-038-C).
   Some of the cylinders in this collection are only of
fair or poor quality because of the sound distortion
created by a warped edge or core. A clearer fidelity may
be found in the recordings in collection 59-002-F.

83-900-F. Elsie Worthington Clews Parsons [?], 1921.
   United States
     Taos Indians
       New York, New York City
         Unknown subjects

Number of cylinders: 5

Number of strips: 5
Sound quality of strips: F 5.
Degree of restriction: 2

   These recordings of Antonio Lujan and John Marcos were
made at the American Museum of Natural History in 1921.
George Herzog recorded Lujan in 1927 (see 54-138-F).
Lujan, a popular Taos performer, was also recorded by Carl
Van Vechten and Leopold Stokowski in the 1920s.

83-901-F. Unknown collector, no date.
     United States
        Hopi Indians
          [Arizona]
            Unknown subjects

Number of cylinders: 15
Number of strips: 15
Sound quality of strips: VP 12, U 3.
Degree of restriction: 1

   This is a minimally documented collection of Hopi Indian
material. The culture group designation was derived from
slips of paper found inside the original cylinder boxes.
   All of the recordings are barely audible.

83-902-C. Simon J. Bronner, donor, ca. 1910-1925.
     United States
        Americans
          Columbia Recording Labs
            Music, Popular
          Edison Recording Labs
            Music, Popular
          [Edision Recording Labs]
            Instrumental music
          Unknown locations
            Unknown subjects

Number of cylinders: 18
Number of strips: 18
Sound quality of strips: G 2,   F 9,   P 6,   B 1.
Degree of restriction: 1

   These commercial cylinders are mainly produced by the
Edison recording labs; others are produced by Columbia
records. The documentation has been compiled from
cylinder rim etchings and from recorded announcements.
   The types of popular music performed include coon songs,
march music, waltzes, two-steps, and quartets.

83-903-F. Unknown collector, no date.
   Unknown countries
      Unknown culture groups
         Unknown locations
            Flute music; Unknown subjects

Number of cylinders: 16
Number of strips: 16
Sound quality of strips: G 3, F 15, P 2, VP 1.
Degree of restriction: 1

   This group of recordings remains, for the most part, a
mystery. The recording technicians for the Cylinder
Project identified a few instruments, such as flutes and a
mbira. A suggestion has been made that several of the
recordings "sound African."

83-904-F. Unknown collector, no date.
   Unknown countries
      Unknown culture groups
         Unknown locations
            Unknown subjects

Number of cylinders: 13
Number of strips: 13
Sound quality of strips: G 11, B 2.
Degree of restriction: 1

   These cylinders contain practically no documentation.
The cylinders sound as though they are from the same
collection and all of the performances are of a solo male
singer. Seven of the songs contain a drum accompaniment.

83-905-F/C. Unknown collector, ca. 1910-1925.
   United States
      Americans
         Edison Recording Labs
            Stories, narratives and anecdotes
   Unknown countries
      Unknown culture groups
         Unknown locations
            Unknown subjects

Number of cylinders: 7
Number of strips: 61
Sound quality of strips: G 1, VP 60.
Degree of restriction: 1

   Of these seven cylinders, the first five appear to be a
separate unit, as the collector's identifying letters are
consecutive ("A" through "E"); the recordings themselves,
however, offer no further information, as they are all of
very poor sound quality. The final two cylinders contain
a commercial recording, "Uncle Josh," and an unidentified

North American Indian song, respectively.

83-906-F. John William Lloyd, 1903.
    United States
       Pima Indians
          [Arizona]
             Corn songs; Flute songs; Tobacco songs; Unknown
             subjects

Number of cylinders: 12
Number of strips: 12
Sound quality of strips: F 7,   P 5.
Degree of restriction: 2

    These cylinders were deposited in the Archives by George
Eager, Museum of the American Indian, New York in 1983.
The documentation for the collection has been gathered
from typed notes found inside the original cylinder boxes.

Reference:
Lloyd, John William. Aw-aw-tam Indian Nights, Being the
Myths and Legends of the Pima of Arizona. Westfield,
N.J.: Lloyd Group, 1911.

83-908-F. George Bird Grinnell [?] or Edward Henry
           Harriman[?], 1899.
    United States
       Tlingit Indians
          Alaska, Orca Station
             Stories, narratives and anecdotes
       Unknown culture groups
          Alaska
             Wolf songs

Number of cylinders: 2
Number of strips: 2
Sound quality of strips: F 2.
Degree of restriction: 2

    The two recordings which constitute this collection were
made on two very unusual cylinders--Columbia Grand
Records. They are very soft, due to a high wax content,
and are each approximately five inches in diameter. These
were deposited in the Archives of Traditional Music by
George Eager, Museum of the American Indian, New York
City.
    There is no definitive evidence as to which member of
the Harriman Alaska Expedition recorded these cylinders.
The researcher is referred to the following publication:
Goetzmann, William H. and Kay Sloan. Looking Far North:
The Harriman Expedition to Alaska, 1899. (New York:
Viking Press, 1982.)
    In order to make a tape of these recordings, a Columbia
Graphophone in good working order had to be located. The

Cylinder Project was very fortunate to find one only
seventeen miles away from Indiana University, at the
Midwest Phonograph Museum, in Martinsville, Indiana. The
cylinders were re-recorded in the Museum on May 11, 1984.
   One of the recordings is a narrative, a story in the
Tlingit language about a man who drowned from the steamer
Wildcat. The second is labeled "Wolf Song," and is
performed by a male with no accompaniment.
   Michael Krauss of the University of Alaska, Fairbanks,
provided assistance in documenting these recordings.

83-909-F. Unknown collector, ca. 1933.
   Unknown countries
      Indians of North American (unidentified)
         Unknown locations
            Unknown subjects
      Unknown culture groups
         Unknown locations
            Unknown subjects

Number of cylinders: 11
Number of strips: 12
Sound quality of strips: F 11, VP 1.
Degree of restriction: 2

   This is an incomplete collection of undocumented large
cylinders. The only indication that these are North
American Indian materials has come from the sound of the
material itself; ten cylinders contain narratives in an
unidentified North American Indian language. On the
remaining cylinder, possibly a test cylinder, a man reads
news about Cordell Hull, then Secretary of State.

83-910-F. Unknown collector, no date.
   Unknown countries
      Unknown culture groups
         Unknown locations
            Unknown subjects

Number of cylinders: 2
Number of strips: 4
Sound quality of strips: G 3, P 1.
Degree of restriction: 1

   These recordings lack any useful documentation. Both
cylinders contain performances by an unaccompanied male
singer.

83-911-F. Guy Benton Johnson, 1928.
   United States
      Afro-Americans
         North Carolina, Chapel Hill
            Blues; Children's game songs; Folk-songs;

Spirituals (Songs); Unknown subjects

Number of cylinders: 8
Number of strips: 30
Sound quality of strips: F 2, P 20, VP 7, U 1.
Degree of restriction: 1

This is an incomplete collection. The documentation for
these recordings has been gathered from collector's notes
found inside the original cylinder boxes and from careful
evaluation of the songs themselves.
A group called Shadrack and Company gives lively
renditions of such spirituals as "My Lord's Gettin'
Ready," "Reign Master Jesus," "Wasn't that a Mighty Day
When Jesus Christ was Born," and "Mary, Don't you Weep."
They also perform secular songs, such as "John Henry" and
"Texas Blues."

83-913-F. Unknown collector, no date.
   Unknown countries
      Unknown culture groups
         Unknown locations
            Unknown subjects

Number of cylinders: 3
Number of strips: 5
Sound quality of strips: G 4, VP 1.
Degree of restriction: 2

These large cylinders contain practically no
documentation other than the comment, "found with Speck
AMNH," written on the original cylinder boxes.
The Cylinder Project technicians report that the singer
for all three recordings seems to be the same person.

83-914-F. John Wight Chapman, 1925.
   United States
      Eskimos
         Alaska, Anvik
            Stories, narratives and anecdotes; Unknown
            subjects
   [United States]
      Unknown culture groups
         [Alaska]
            Unknown subjects

Number of cylinders: 7
Number of strips: 17
Sound quality of strips: F 10, P 7.
Degree of restriction: 2

This collection was previously unidentified. However,
the Cylinder Project recording technicians found that one
of the cylinders contained a lengthy narrative from J. W.

Chapman himself, a fascinating "long distance message" which gave much ethnographic information. Included were the collector's name, the location of the recording and the date. This narrative has been transcribed by Bruce Harrah-Conforth and Nancy Cassell; the text is a part of the documentation for this collection.

One of the recordings contains songs by James Fox. The other recordings are narratives.

Reference:
Chapman, John Wight. Ten'a Texts and Tales from Anvik, Alaska. Leyden: E.J. Brill Limited, 1914.

83-915-F. Unknown collector, no date.
   Unknown countries
      Unknown culture groups
         Unknown locations
            Unknown subjects

Number of cylinders: 2
Number of strips: 2
Sound quality of strips: G 1, VP 1.
Degree of restriction: 1

   These cylinders lack documentation of any sort.

83-916-F. Unknown collector, no date.
   Unknown countries
      Indians of North American (unidentified)
         Unknown locations
            Unknown subjects
      Unknown culture groups
         Unknown locations
            Unknown subjects

Number of cylinders: 21
Number of strips: 21
Sound quality of strips: F 12, P 8, VP 1.
Degree of restriction: 2

   These cylinders cannot be identified by any information other than the fact that they sound like North American Indian songs. There is no valid documentation for this collection.
   Some of the songs are accompanied by a shaken idiophone, possibly a rattle. Most are performed by one male singer. There are a few narratives.

83-917-F. Franz Boas and John Comfort Fillmore, 1893 [?],
            or Franz Boas and Julie Averkieva, 1930 [?].
   United States or Canada
      Kwakiutl Indians
         Unknown locations

        Unknown subjects

Number of cylinders: 76
Number of strips: 88
Sound quality of strips: G 1, F 67, VP 1, B 6, U 13.
Degree of restriction: 2

    There is some confusion surrounding the origin of these
large galvano-plastic cylinder copies. It is possible
that some of these cylinders were recorded at the World's
Columbian Exposition in Chicago, 1893, where Franz Boas
was the organizer of a reproduction of a Kwakiutl village.
    Present documentation for the collection was compiled
from notes on the original cylinder boxes. The informants
are many; most of the selections are sung by a solo male
and are accompanied by a percussion instrument.
    Warping of the plastic cylinders has resulted in some
cases of snags, distortions and unplayable selections.

References:
Boas, Franz. The Social Organization and Secret Societies
of the Kwakiutl Indians, 1895 Report of the U.S. National
Museum, published by the Smithsonian Institution, 1897;
reprint edition, New York City: Johnson Reprint Corp.,
1970.

_____. "Songs of the Kwakiutl," Internationale
Archiv für Ethnographie, Supplement to Vol. IX
(1896):1-9.

_____. "Sixth Report on the Indians of British
Columbia," 1896 Report of the British Association for the
Advancement of Science, London: John Murray, Spotiswoode
and Co., 1896, p. 569-591.

_____. Kwakiutl Ethnography, Helen Codere, ed.,
Chicago: University of Chicago Press, 1966.

Related collections: 54-121-F; 54-035-F.

83-918-F. George Herzog, ca. 1930-1931.
    Liberia
      Jabo (African people)
        Unknown locations
          Unknown subjects; Vocabulary and
          pronunciation [?]

Number of cylinders: 16
Number of strips: 137
Sound quality of strips: F 38, P 55, VP 44.
Degree of restriction: 1

    This collection of large cylinders appears to be
complete. There is no documentation for the collection

other than the culture group designation, written on the
original cylinder boxes.
   Most of these recordings are spoken by one male voice;
the subject matter could be language lessons. The voice
does not seem to be George Herzog's. The speaker might
well be Charles Blooah, who accompanied Herzog on the
Liberian field trip--to Blooah's home village--and
instructed him in the Jabo language.
   Four of the cylinders contain recordings of unidentified
songs. All of the recordings begin with the sound of a
pitch pipe (A-440).

83-919-F. Unknown collector, 1927 and ca. 1930.
   United States
      Cochiti Indians
         New Mexico, Pueblo Cochiti
            Buffalo dance songs
      Unknown countries
      Unknown culture groups
         Unknown locations
            Unknown subjects

Number of cylinders: 5
Number of strips: 10
Sound quality of strips: F 4, P 5, U 1.
Degree of restriction: 2

   Each of these five cylinders, received from the American
Museum of Natural History, has separate identification.
   SCY 4862 The cylinder announcement is as follows: "Four
Buffalo dance songs, sung by ___ Pima, Cochiti Indian boy,
5 years old, at Pueblo Cochiti, New Mexico, May 5th, 1927,
recorded under the direction of Alice [?] Barrington [?]."
   SCY 4868 This may be a test cylinder: it contains
several popular English songs.
   SCY 4869 This may be a test cylinder: it contains two
renditions of "The Farmer in the Dell."
   SCY 4870 Missing.
   SCY 4871 Unidentified. The instruments played on the
recording are membranophones, gongs, and chordophones.
There is also singing.

83-921-F. Unknown collector, ca. 1930.
   United States
      Indians of North America (unidentified)
         Unknown locations
            Unknown subjects
      Unknown culture groups
         Unknown locations
            Unknown subjects

Number of cylinders: 12
Number of strips: 12
Sound quality of strips: G 2, F 4, P 1, VP 3, B 2.

Degree of restriction: 2

   Some of these cylinders apparently came from the Field
Museum of Natural History, Chicago, but there is no clear
documentation of their contents.
   Four of the cylinders were broken, and repaired by the
Cylinder Project technicians. These are playable, but of
poor sound quality.

83-922-C. Unknown depositor, ca. 1910-1925.
   United States
      Americans
         Edison Recording Labs
            Music, Popular; Stories, narratives and
            anecdotes; War songs
      Scots
         Edison Recording Labs
            Music, Popular
   Unknown countries
      Unknown culture groups
         Unknown locations
            Unknown subjects

Number of cylinders: 20
Number of strips: 20
Sound quality of strips: G 5, F 2, P 1, U 12.
Degree of restriction: 1

   As is the case with many commercial cylinders, the
documentation has been derived mainly from the
inscriptions on the edges of the cylinders themselves;
these inscriptions include the name of the band and the
song title. In a few cases, the title of the composition
is also announced on the cylinder recording.
   These cylinders contain a variety of American popular
songs, a Scottish popular song, jokes and anecdotes, and
several World War I songs. Many are group performances,
and most also have the accompaniment of an orchestra or a
band.

83-923-F. Unknown collector, no date.
   Unknown countries
      Unknown culture groups
         Unknown locations
            Unknown subjects

Number of cylinders: 3
Number of strips: 13
Sound quality of strips: G 4, P 9.
Degree of restriction: 3

   These cylinders lack any useful documentation.

85-440-C. Glenn Simonelli, donor, 1985.
    United States
        Americans
            Edison Recording Labs
                Stories, narratives and anecdotes

Number of cylinders: 2
Number of strips: 2
Sound quality of strips: G 1, F 1.
Degree of restriction: 1

    These cylinders are stories about "Uncle Josh" recorded
by Cal Stewart.

Index of Names

Including collectors, informants (inf.), performers (perf.), donors, expeditions, expositions, and recording companies.

Adamson, Thelma.
    54-043-F: 1930, Washington (State); Nooksack
        Indians
    54-130-F: 1927, Washington (State); Chehalis
        Indians
    54-131-F: 1927, Washington (State); Chehalis
        Indians
    54-133-F: 1927, Washington (State); Various Indian
        groups

Afraid of Hawk, Edward. See Edward Afraid of Hawk

Albanez, Jose Luis. (inf.)   54-123-F

Altman, Patricia. (inf.)   69-015-F

Altman, Ralph C. (inf.)   69-015-F

Andrade, Manuel Jose.
    83-892-F: 1928, United States; Quileute Indians

Angulo, Jaime de.
    54-013-F: 1925, California; Achomawi Indians

Arms, Charlie. (inf.)   54-025-F

Averkieva, Julie.
    54-035-F: 1893 and 1930, British Columbia; Kwakiutl
        Indians
    83-917-F: 1893 or 1930, United States or Canada;
        Kwakiutl Indians

Azul, Roy. (inf.)   54-228-F

Badrobe, Tom. (inf.)   54-025-F

Barrett, Samuel Alfred.
     54-098-F: 1905-1908, Oregon and California; Various
              Indian groups
     63-42-F: 1911, Arizona; Hopi Indians

Bear Child. (inf.)   54-096-F

Beckwith, Martha Warren.
     54-147-F: 1921, Jamaica

Berlin Phonogramm-Archiv.
     59-002-F: 1900-1913; World
     83-899-F: 1900-1913; World

Blackbird, Ed. (inf.)   54-025-F

Blackbird, Thick. (inf.)   54-025-F

Black-Looks. (inf.)   54-095-F

Blooah, Charles. (inf.)   83-819-F

Boaz, Franz.
     54-035-F: 1893 and 1930, British Columbia; Kwakiutl
              Indians
     54-121-F: 1893, Chicago; Kwakiutl Indians
     54-131-F: 1927, Washington (State); Chehalis
              Indians
     54-139-F: 1897, British Columbia; Ntlakyapamuk
              Indians
     83-917-F: 1893 or 1930, United States or Canada;
              Kwakiutl Indians

Bogoras, Waldemar.
     54-149-F: 1901-1902, Soviet Union, Siberia

Bogoraz, Vladimir Germanovich. See Bogoras, Waldemar

Bronner, Simon J. (donor)   83-902-C

Brooks, Bill. (inf.)   54-097-F

Brow Leather. (inf.)   54-136-F

Bull Child. (inf.)   54-096-F

Burlin, Natalie Curtis.
     54-027-F: 1903, Arizona; Hopi Indians
     54-065-F: 1915-1918, Virginia; Africans
     54-118-F: 1903, Arizona; Various Indian groups
     54-145-F: 1917, Virginia; Afro-Americans

Cape, Jim. (inf.)   54-128-F

Carter, Jim. (inf.)   54-124-F

Chandler, Milford G.
      54-196-F: 1926, United States; Winnebago Indians

Chapman, John Wight.
      83-914-F: 1925, Alaska; Eskimos

Chews-Black-Bones. (inf.)   54-095-F

Chief Deskáheh. See General, Alexander J.

Chopwood, Henry. (inf.)   54-017-F

Clews, Elsie Worthington. See Parsons, Elsie Worthington
      Clews

Cloud, Leslie. (inf.)   54-107-F

Cohen, Felix S.
      54-017-F: 1930, Montana; Assiniboin Indians
      54-025-F: 1930, Montana; Atsina Indians

Cole, Fay-Cooper.
      54-079-F: 1907-1908, Philippines

Cole, Madikane. (inf.)   54-065-F

Coleman, Kate. (inf.)   54-114-F

Collier, Robert. (inf.)   54-034-F

Columbia Recording Labs.
      69-015-F/C, 75-199-C, 80-084-C, 80-085-C, 83-889-C,
      83-902-C

Comer, George.
      54-115-F: 1903-1909, Northwest Territories; Eskimos

Cozad, Bilo. (inf.)   54-031-F

Crocker Land Expedition (1913-1917).
      54-116-F: 1917, Northwest Territories; Eskimos

Croff, Sadie. (inf.)   54-025-F

Cross-Guns. (inf.)   54-095-F

Cuervas, Salvador. (inf.)   54-123-F

Curtis, Edward S.
      57-014-F: 1907-1913, United States and Canada;
            Various Indian groups

Curtis-Burlin, Natalie. See Burlin, Natalie Curtis

Davis, Marion. (inf.)   54-130-F, 54-131-F

De Angulo, Jaime. See Angulo, Jaime de

De Dios, Juan. See Dios, Juan de

Deskáheh. See General, Alexander J.

Diego, Juan. (inf.)   54-042-F

Dios, Juan de. (inf.)   54-123-F

Dives Backwards. (inf.)   54-104-F

Dixon, Joseph Kossuth.
    54-094-F: 1909, Montana; Siksika Indians
    54-102-F: 1909, Montana; Apache Indians
    54-108-F: 1909, Montana; Crow Indians
    54-109-F: 1909, Montana; Dakota Indians

Dixon, Roland Burrage.
    54-097-F: 1910, California; Maidu Indians

Dorsey, George Amos.
    54-010-F: 1899, British Columbia; Kwakiutl Indians
    54-011-F: 1902, United States; Pawnee Indians
    54-044-F: 1902, Oklahoma; Various Indian groups
    54-045-F: 1906, Oklahoma; Pawnee Indians
    54-047-F: 1906, Chicago; Chinese
    54-078-F: 1906, Chicago; Igorot
    54-192-F: 1905, United States; Pawnee Indians

Dowington, Dick. (inf.)   54-013-F

Dubois, Constance Goddard.
    54-113-F: 1905, California; Diegueño Indians
    54-123-F: 1906, California; Liesueño Indians

Edison Military Band. (perf.)   80-086-C

Edison Recording Labs.
    54-094-C, 54-102-C, 54-108-C, 54-109-C, 80-084-C,
    80-085-C, 80-086-F, 83-889-C, 83-902-F, 83-905-F/C,
    83-922-C

Edward Afraid of Hawk. (inf.)   54-110-F

Emeneau, Murray Barnson.
    54-080-F: 1938, India

Evans, Mary. (inf.)   54-095-F

Everts, Mark. (inf.)   54-051-F

Eyley, Mrs. Sam. (inf.)   54-133-F

Eyley, Sam. (inf.)   54-133-F

Farrand, Livingston.
          54-127-F: 1898, Washington (State); Quileute
                Indians
          54-128-F: 1898, Washington (State); Quinault
                Indians

Fenton, William Nelson.
          54-028-F: 1933, New York; Seneca Indians

Fillmore, John Comfort.
          54-035-F: [1893?] and 1930, British Columbia;
                Kwakiutl Indians
          54-121-F: 1893, Chicago; Kwakiutl Indians
          83-917-F: 1893 or 1930, United States or Canada;
                Kwakiutl Indians

Firstshoot, Simon. (inf.)   54-017-F

Flying, Rex. (inf.)   54-017-F

Fox, James. (inf.)   83-914-F

Gardner, Frank. (inf.)   64-040-F

Gardner, Rose. (inf.)   64-040-F

General, Alexander J.
          54-029-F: 1928, Ontario; Cayuga Indians

Gillis, Frank J. (donor)   80-084-C

Goddard, Pliny Earle.
          54-103-F: 1909-1910, 1914, Arizona, New Mexico;
                Various Indian groups
          54-136-F: 1905 ca., Alberta; Sarsi Indians

Goddard-Dubois, Constance. See Dubois, Constance Goddard

Good Bird. (inf.)   54-117-F

Good Road. (inf.)   54-117-F

Grasshopper. (inf.)   54-136-F

Grinnell, George Bird.
          54-095-F: 1897, Montana; Siksika Indians
          54-104-F: 1897-1898, Montana; Cheyenne Indians
          83-908-F: 1899, Alaska; Tlingit Indians

Gunther, Erna.
          54-034-F: 1925, Washington (State); Clallam Indians

Ha-ta-kek. (inf.)   54-123-F

Haas, Mary Rosamond.
        54-009-F: 1933, United States and Louisiana;
              Various Indian groups

Haeberlin, Herman Karl.
        54-132-F: 1917, Washington (State); Salish Indians

Haimasela, Tom. (inf.)   54-010-F

Halpert, Herbert.
        83-889-C
        83-890-F: 1930, New Jersey; Americans

Hambly, Wilfrid Dyson.
        54-007-F: 1929-1930, Angola; Mbundu (African
              people)

Hambopolo. (inf.)   60-019-F

Hampton Quartette. (perf.)   54-145-F

Hanks, Jane Richardson.
        54-019-F: 1938-1939, Alberta; Siksika Indians
        54-031-F: 1935, Oklahoma; Kiowa Indians

Harriman, Edward Henry.
        83-908-F: 1899, Alaska; Tlingit Indians

Harriman Alaska Expedition (1899).
        83-908-F

Hasse, John Edward. (donor)   80-085-C

Head Above Water, Jack. See Jack Head Above Water

Henry, Jules.
        54-014-F: 1933, New Mexico; Mescalero Indians

Herskovits, Frances Shapiro.
        67-151-F: 1928-1929, Haiti and Surinam
        67-152-F: 1931, Ghana and Nigeria

Herskovits, Melville Jean.
        67-151-F: 1928-1929, Haiti and Surinam
        67-152-F: 1931, Ghana and Nigeria

Heruska, Dave. (inf.)   54-099-F

Herzog, George.
        54-101-F: 1927, New Mexico; Acoma Indians
        54-106-F: 1927, New Mexico; Cochiti Indians
        54-110-F: 1928, North Dakota; Dakota Indians
        54-114-F: 1927, California; Diegueño Indians
        54-119-F: 1928, New York; Hopi Indians
        54-120-F: 1927, California; Hupa Indians
        54-122-F: 1927, New Mexico; Laguna Indians

        54-124-F: 1927, Arizona; Mohave Indians
        54-126-F: 1927, Arizona; Pima Indians
        54-129-F: 1927, New Mexico; San Ildefonso Indians
        54-134-F: 1927, Arizona and New Mexico; San Juan
           ·Indians
        54-137-F: 1927, California; Serrano Indians
        54-138-F: 1927, New Mexico; Taos Indians
        54-142-F: 1927, Arizona; Yuma Indians
        54-144-F: 1927, New Mexico; Zuñi Indians
        54-223-F: 1930-1931, Liberia; Jabo (African people)
        54-224-F: 1929, Chicago; Jabo (African people)
        54-228-F: 1929, Arizona; Pima and Maricopa Indians
        83-895-F: 1927, New Mexico; San Juan Indians
        83-918-F: 1930-1931, Liberia; Jabo (African people)

Hills, Frank. (inf.)   54-142-F

Hoops, Isaac P. (inf.)   64-040-F

Hornbostel, Erich M. von.
        54-045-F: 1906, Oklahoma; Pawnee Indians
        54-078-F: 1906, Chicago; Igorot
        59-002-F: Berlin Phonogramm-Archiv Demonstration
           Collection
        83-899-F: Berlin Phonogramm-Archiv Demonstration
           Collection

Howard, Victoria. (inf.)   54-185-F

Hunt, Joe. (inf.)   54-133-F

Hunt, Mary. (inf.)   54-133-F

Hunting Horse, Monroe. See Monroe Hunting Horse

Hurley, Frank. See Hurley, James Francis

Hurley, James Francis.
        54-142-F: 1921, New Guinea

Iokelson, Vladimir Ilich. See Jochelson, Waldemar

Jack Head Above Water. (inf.)   54-136-F

Jackson Street Theater Band. (perf.)   54-047-F

Jacob H. Schiff Chinese Expedition (1901-1904).
        54-140-F

Jacobs, Melville.
        54-133-F: 1929-1930, Washington (State); Various
           Indian groups
        54-185-F: 1929-1930, Oregon; Clackamas Indians

James, Albert. (inf.)   54-228-F

Jesup North Pacific Expedition (1897-1903).
     54-139-F, 54-149-F

Jochelson, Waldemar.
     54-149-F: 1901-1902, Soviet Union, Sibera

Johnson, Guy Benton.
     83-911-F: 1928, North Carolina; Afro-Americans

Johnson, Joe. (inf.)   54-034-F

Jones, William.
     54-105-F: 1903-1905, Minnesota; Chippewa Indians

Kabitcimala. See   Cloud, Leslie

Kamba-Simango, Columbus.   See   Simango, Columbus Kamba

Kapohaialii, Lucy. (inf.)   54-206-F

Kayatyci. (inf.)   54-122-F

Kroeber, Alfred Louis.
     54-098-F: 1905-1908, Oregon, California; Various
          Indian groups

Kroeber, Henrietta.
     54-098-F: 1905-1908, Oregon, California; Various
          Indian groups

Kuhi, P. K. (inf.)   54-206-F

Laman, Karl Edvard.
     54-210-F: 1913-1922, Congo; Bakongo (African
          people)
     54-211-F: 1913-1922, French Equatorial Africa; Teke
          (African people)

Laguna Jim. (inf.)   54-123-F

Laufer, Bethold.
     54-076-F: 1908, India
     54-150-F: 1901-1902, China

Laves, Gerhardt Kurt.
     54-077-F: 1930, Australia; Karadjeri

Lesser, Alexander.
     54-051-F: 1930, United States; Pawnee and Wichita
          Indians

Lipkind, William.
        54-053-F: 1938, Brazil; Caraja and Cayapo Indians

Little Head. (inf.)   54-104-F

Lloyd, John William.
        83-906-F: 1903, Arizona; Pima Indians

Lopez, Juan. (inf.)   54-042-F

Lopez, Patricio. (inf.)   54-042-F

Luhan, Tony. See Lujan, Antonio

Lujan, Antonio. (inf.)   54-138-F, 83-900-F

Lumholtz, Carl.
        54-092-F: 1898, Mexico; Tarahumare Indians
        54-093-F: 1898, Mexico; Huichol Indians

Lumholtz, Karl Sofus. See Lumholtz, Carl

MacMeanman, Paohraic. (inf.)   60-026-F

Marcos, John. (inf.)   83-900-F

Maristo, Santiago. (inf.)   54-042-F

Martínez, Sam. (inf.)   54-138-F

Mason, John Alden.
        54-052-F: 1923, Colombia; Arhuaco Indians
        54-054-F: 1923, Colombia; Goajiro Indians
        54-148-F: 1914-1915, Puerto Rico

Matthews, Washington.
        54-125-F: 1893-1901, Arizona and New Mexico; Navaho
                Indians

Monroe Hunting Horse. (inf.)   54-031-F

Morongo, Rose. (inf.)   54-137-F

Morey, Robert H.
        54-003-F: 1935, Liberia

Murie, James R.
        54-011-F: 1902, United States; Pawnee Indians
        54-044-F: 1902, Oklahoma[?]; Various Indian groups
        54-192-F: 1905, United States; Pawnee Indians

Nordland Exposition (1911: Berlin).
        59-002-F, 83-899-F

O'Duilearga, Séamus.
     60-026-F: 1930 ca., Ireland

Old Man Horse. (inf.)   54-031-F

Opler, Morris Edward.
     54-014-F: 1933, New Mexico; Mescalero Indians

Packs Wolf. (inf.)   54-117-F

Paikula, K. (inf.)   54-206-F

Pancho, Jose. (inf.)   54-042-F

Pancho, Juan. (inf.)   54-042-F

Park, Willard Zerbe.
     54-191-F: 1934, United States; Paiute Indians

Parsons, Elsie Worthington Clews.
     54-143-F: 1925, United States; Zuñi Indians
     54-146-F: 1920, Jamaica
     83-900-F: 1921, New York; Taos Indians

Pecos, Epífhano. (inf.)   54-106-F

Pẽna, Antonio. (inf.)   54-129-F

Pina, Mrs. (inf.)   54-122-F

Radin, Paul.
     54-140-F: 1908, Nebraska; Various Indian groups

Reeves, K. (inf.)   54-097-F

Reichard, Gladys Amanda.
     54-039-F: 1938, United States; Navaho Indians

Rex Flying. See Flying, Rex

Richardson-Hanks, Jane. See Hanks, Jane Richardson

Rides-at-the-Door. (inf.)   54-095-F

Roberts, Helen Heffron.
     54-146-F: 1920, Jamaica
     54-147-F: 1921, Jamaica
     54-206-F: 1923, Hawaii

Sapir, Edward.
     54-041-F: 1910, 1913-1914, Canada; Nitinat Indians
     60-017-F: 1910, United States; Various Indian

groups
[83-897-F?]

Schiff Expedition to China. See Jacob H. Schiff Chinese
    Expedition (1901-1904)

Schultz, James Willard.
    64-040-F: 1926, Canada; Siksika Indians

Seneca, Dan. (inf.)   54-130-F

Seneca, Mrs. Dan. (inf.)   54-130-F

Shadrack and Company (Musical group).   83-911-F

Shapiro-Herskovits, Frances. See Herskovits, Frances
    Shapiro

Shotridge, Louis.
    83-896-F: 1910, United States; Various Indian
        groups

Simango, Columbus Kamba. (inf.)   54-065-F

Simonelli, Glenn. (donor)   85-440-F

Sitcó'm·á·ì. (inf.)   54-124-F

Speck, Frank Gouldsmith.
    54-029-F: 1928, Ontario; Cayuga Indians
    54-107-F: 1905, Oklahoma; Creek and Shawnee Indians
    54-141-F: 1905, Oklahoma; Creek and Yuchi Indians
    60-018-F: 1905-1911, United States or Canada;
        Various Indian groups

Spencer, D. S.
    54-097-F: 1910, California; Maidu Indians

Spier, Leslie.
    54-033-F: 1935, Oregon; Klamath Indians

Spinden, Herbert Joseph.
    54-135-F: 1912, New Mexico; Nambé and Santa Clara
        Indians

Starr, Frederick A.
    69-015-F/C: 1906, Zaire
    75-199-C: 1910-1912, United States

Starr, George. (inf.)   54-095-F

Stewart, Cal. (inf.)   85-440-C

Stewart, Frank. (inf.)   64-040-F

Stewart, Jack. (inf.)   64-040-F

Stumbling Bear. (inf.)   54-031-F

Subish, Margarita. (inf.)   54-123-F

Suina, Ruys. (inf.)   54-106-F

Swadesh, Morris.
      54-009-F: 1933, United States and Louisiana;
             Various Indian groups
      54-041-F: 1931, Canada; Nitinat Indians

Talks Different. (inf.)   54-017-F

Tan-Bogoraz, Vladimir Germanovich. See Bogoras, Waldemar

Teit, James Alexander.
      54-139-F: 1897, British Columbia; Ntlakyapamuk
             Indians

Thurnwald, Richard.
      83-891-F: 1933, Melanesia

Tiger, Jim. (inf.)   54-141-F

Tillohash, Tony. (inf.)   60-017-F

Underhill, Ruth Murray.
      54-042-F: 1931, 1933, United States; Papago Indians

Vanyiko, Thomas. (inf.)   54-126-F, 54-228-F

Voegelin, Charles Frederick.
      54-181-F: 1935, Oklahoma; Shawnee Indians

Voegelin, Erminie Wheeler. See Wheeler-Voegelin, Erminie

von Hornbostel, Erich M. See Hornbostel, Erich M. von

Wagley, Charles.
      54-055-F: 1935, Brazil; Caraja and Tapirapé
             Indians

Walker, James John.
      54-112-F: 1908, South Dakota; Dakota Indians

Wanamaker Historical Expedition (2nd: 1909).
      54-094-F, 54-102-F, 54-108-F, 54-109-F

Watc'i'bidiza. (inf.)   54-110-F

Wawhee, Dick. (inf.)   54-013-F

Weltfish, Gene.
        54-051-F: 1930, United States; Pawnee and Wichita
            Indians

Wheeler-Voegelin, Erminie.
        54-181-F: 1935, Oklahoma; Shawnee Indians

White Calf, James. (inf.)   54-095-F

White Horse. (inf.)   54-031-F

White, Leslie A.
        54-101-F: 1927, New Mexico; Acoma Indians
        60-004-F: 1927-1928, New Mexico; Various Indian
            groups

Wild Hog. (inf.)   54-104-F

Wilson, Gilbert Livingstone.
        54-117-F: 1906-1909, United States; Hidatsa and
            Mandan Indians

Wing Gray. (inf.)   54-017-F

Wipes His Eyes. (inf.)   54-095-F

Wissler, Clark.
        54-096-F: 1903-1904, Alberta, Montana; Piegan and
            Siksika Indians

World's Columbian Exposition (1893: Chicago, Ill.).
        54-035-F, 54-121-F, 83-917-F

Xwan, Jonas. (inf.)   54-130-F

Young, Sam. (inf.)   54-009-F

Young, Ti. (inf.)   54-097-F

Index of Culture Groups

Similar spellings are indicated by { }.

Abnaki Indians. 60-018-F

Aborigines, Australian. See Australian Aborigines

Absaroka Indians {Absahrokee}. See Crow Indians

Achomawi Indians. 54-013-F

Acoma Indians. 54-101-F, 57-014-F, 60-004-F

Africans. 54-065-F

Afro-Americans. 54-145-F, 83-911-F

Aivilingmiuts. See Eskimos

Alfures {Alfuros}. 59-002-F, 83-899-F

Algonquian Indians {Algonkian}. 60-018-F

American Indians (unidentified). See Indians of North
  America (unidentified)

Americans. 54-041-F, 75-199-C, 80-084-C, 80-085-C,
  80-086-C, 83-889-C, 83-890-F, 83-902-C, 83-905-C,
  83-922-C, 85-440-C

Anglo-Americans. See British Americans

Angoni. 83-899-F

Anishinabe Indians. See Chippewa Indians

Aonas. See Ona Indians

Apache Indians. 54-102-C, 54-103-F

Apayao {Apoyao}. See Isneg

Apsaroke Indians. See Crow Indians

Arapaho Indians {Arapahoe}. 54-044-F, 57-014-F

Arecuna Indians {Arekuna}. 59-002-F, 83-899-F

Arhuaco Indians {Aruaco}. 54-052-F

Arikara Indians {Arickara, Arickaree}. 54-044-F,
    54-110-F, 57-014-F

Asantes (African people) {Asantis}. See Ashantis
    (African people)

Ashantis (African people) {Ashantees}. 67-152-F

Asiarmiuts. See Eskimos

Assiniboin Indians. 54-017-F, 59-002-F, 83-899-F

Athapascan Indians {Athabascan}. 83-896-F

Atsina Indians. 54-025-F, 57-014-F

Australian Aborigines. 59-002-F, 83-899-F

Babwende (Bantu people) {Babouende, Babuende, Babuanye}
    59-002-F, 83-899-F

Bagobo (Philippine people). 54-079-F

Baguirmi (African people) {Bagirmi}. 59-002-F, 83-899-F

Bakongo (African people). 54-210-F, 59-002-F, 83-899-F

Bakuba (African people). See Kuba (African people)

Balinese (Indonesian people). 59-002-F, 83-899-F

Baluba (African people). See Luba (African people)

Bamum (African people) {Bamoun, Bamun}. 59-002-F,
    83-899-F

Bandi (African people). See Gbandi (African people)

Bangi (African people). 69-015-C

Banguella (Bantu people). See Ngangela (Bantu people)

Basiba (African people). See Haya (African people)

Batak (Palawan people). 54-079-F

Bateke (African people). See Teke (African people)

Baziba (African people). See Haya (African people)

Bengalis {Bengalese}. 54-076-F

Benguella (Bantu people). See Ngangela (Bantu people)

Beothuk Indians {Beothikan, Beothukan}. 60-018-F

Berbers (Moroccan). 59-002-F

Bilaan (Philippine people). 54-079-F

Bimbundu (African people). See Mbundu (African people)

Black Americans. See Afro-Americans

Blackfoot Indians. See Siksika Indians

Blood Indians. See Kainah Indians

Bobangi (African people). See Bangi (African people)

Bondei. See Zigula (Bantu people)

British Americans. 54-034-F, 54-095-F, 54-118-F, 54-140-F

Bukidnon (Philippine people). 54-079-F

Bula (African people). 59-002-F, 83-899-F

Bungi Indians {Bungee}. See Chippewa Indians

Burmese. 59-002-F, 83-899-F

Bushongo (African people). See Kuba (African people)

Byelorussians. 59-002-F, 83-899-F

Calagar. See Kalagan (Philippine people)

Calapooyan Indians. See Kalapuyan Indians

Camanche Indians. See Comanche Indians

Canadians, French. See French-Canadians

Canienga Indians. See Mohawk Indians

Cape Indians. See Makah Indians

Caraja Indians {Carayás}. 54-053-F, 54-055-F

Cayapo Indians. 54-053-F

Cayuga Indians. 54-029-F

Chaga (African people) {Chagga}. 59-002-F, 83-899-F

Chehalis Indians. 54-130-F, 54-131-F

Cherokee Indians. 54-009-F

Cheyenne Indians. 54-044-F, 54-104-F, 54-134-F,
    54-138-F, 57-014-F, 60-017-F

Chickasaw Indians {Chicachas, Chicasa, Chichacha}
    54-141-F

Chinese. 54-047-F, 54-150-F, 59-002-F, 83-899-F

Chinook Indians. 54-133-F

Chippewa Indians {Chippeway}. 54-029-F, 54-100-F,
    54-105-F, 54-140-F

Chiricahua Indians. See Apache Indians

Chopunnish Indians. See Nez Percé Indians

Chukchi {Chuckchee, Chuckchi}. 54-149-F

Chuvashes. 83-899-F

Cingalese. See Sinhalese

Clackamas Indians {Clackama}. 54-185-F

Claiakwat Indians. See Clayoquot Indians

Clallam Indians. 54-034-F

Classet Indians {Clatset}. See Makah Indians

Clayoquot Indians. 57-014-F

Cochiti Indians. 54-106-F, 57-014-F, 83-919-F

Cocomaricopa Indians. See Maricopa Indians

Comanche Indians {Commanche, Commance}. 54-101-F,
    54-106-F, 54-122-F, 54-134-F, 54-135-F, 60-004-F

Cootenai Indians. See Kutenai Indians

Cowichan Indians. 57-014-F

Cowlitz Indians. 54-133-F

Cree Indians. 59-002-F, 83-899-F

Creek Indians. 54-107-F, 54-141-F

Crow Indians. 54-108-C, 54-110-F, 54-140-F, 57-014-F

Cuchan Indians {Cuichana, Cutgana}. See Yuma Indians

Dahomey (African people) {Dahomans, Dahomeans,
  Dahomeyans}. See Fon (African people)

Dakota Indians. 54-109-C, 54-110-F, 54-112-F, 54-140-F,
  83-897-F

Delaware Indians. 54-029-F

Desana Indians. 59-002-F, 83-899-F

Diegueño Indians. 54-113-F, 54-114-F

Djabo (African people). See Jabo (African people)

Djuka (Surinam people). 67-151-F

Dschagga (African people). See Chaga (African people)

Dzalamo (African people). See Wazaramo (African people)

Dzindza (African people). See Zinza (African people)

Ekihaya (African people). See Haya (African people)

Elmoran. See Masai

Engganese (Indonesian people) {Engganos, Enganos}
  59-002-F, 83-899-F

English Americans. See British Americans

Eskimos {Eskimauan Indians, Esquimaux}. 54-115-F,
  54-116-F, 54-149-F, 59-002-F, 83-899-F, 83-914-F

Etchemin Indians. See Malecite Indians

Eton (African people) {Etum}. 59-002-F, 83-899-F

Evenki. See Tunguses

Ewe (African people). 59-002-F, 83-899-F

Ewondo (African people). See Eton (African people)

Fjort (African people). See Bakongo (African people)

Flathead Indians. See Salish Indians

Fon (African people). 60-019-F, 67-152-F

French. 54-140-F

French-Canadians. 60-018-F

Gaingbe (African people). See Mina (African people)

Ganguella (Bantu people). See Ngangela (Bantu people)

Gbandi (African people) {Gbande, Gbassi}. 54-003-F

Ge (African people). See Mina (African people)

Georgians (Transcaucasians). 83-899-F

Germans. 75-199-C

Ghurkas {Ghoorkas}. See Gurkhas

Goajiro Indians. 54-054-F

Gorkhas {Goorkhas}. See Gurkhas

Gros Ventres of Missouri. See Hidatsa Indians

Gros Ventres of Montana. See Atsina Indians

Gros Ventres of the Prairie. See Atsina Indians

Grusinians. See Georgians (Transcaucasians)

Guajiro Indians. See Goajiro Indians

Guingbe (African people). See Mina (African people)

Gujaratis (Indic people) {Gujaratees, Gujratis}. 59-002-F

Gurkhas {Gurkhe}. 83-899-F

Haida Indians. 57-014-F

Haitians. 67-151-F

Hausas {Haussas}. 59-002-F, 83-899-F

Hawaiians. 54-206-F

Haya (African people). 59-002-F, 83-899-F

Heia (African people). See Haya (Africa people)

Hesquiat Indians {Hesquiaht}. 57-014-F

Hidatsa Indians. 54-117-F, 57-014-F

Higaonan (Philippine people). See Bukidnon (Philippine people)

Hindus. 54-076-F

Hisquiat Indians. See Hesquiat Indians

Hoopah Indians. See Hupa Indians

Hopi Indians. 54-027-F, 54-118-F, 54-119-F, 59-002-F, 60-017-F, 63-042-F, 83-899-F, 83-901-F

Hualapai Indians {Hualapi}. 60-017-F

Huichol Indians. 54-093-F, 59-002-F, 83-899-F

Huma Indians. See Yuma Indians

Hupa Indians. 54-120-F

Huron Indians. 60-018-F

Ibernians. See Georgian (Transcaucasians)

Igorot {Igorrotes}. 54-078-F

Ilaoquatsh Indians. See Clayoquot Indians

Indians of North America (unidentified). 54-099-F, 83-893-F, 83-909-F, 83-916-F, 83-921-F

Inuit {Innuit}. See Eskimos

Iraya. See Mangyans (Philippine people)

Irish. 60-026-F

Isneg. 54-079-F

Italians. 83-889-C

Iukagir. See Yukaghir

Jabo (African people). 54-223-F, 54-224-F, 83-918-F

Jagga (African people). See Chaga (African people)

Jamaicans. 54-147-F

Japanese. 59-002-F, 83-899-F

Jaricuna Indians {Jarecoune}. See Arecuna Indians

Javanese. 59-002-F

Jews, Sephardic. See Sephardim

Jicarilla Indians {Jicarilla Apache}. 54-103-F, 54-134-F

Jinja (African people). See Zinza (African people)

Kafirs (African people). See Zulus

Kainah Indians. 54-096-F

Kalagan (Philippine people). 54-079-F

Kalapuyan Indians {Kalapooian}. 54-185-F

Kalingas. 54-079-F

Karadjeri (Australian people). 54-077-F

Karajá Indians. See Caraja Indians

Karok Indians. 54-120-F

Karthveli. See Georgians (Transcaucasians)

Kayapo Indians. See Cayapo Indians

Kennebec Indians. See Abnaki Indians

Keresan Indians. 60-004-F

Kiaknukmiuts {Kiakennuckmiuts}. See Eskimos

Kickapoo Indians {Kikapoo}. 60-017-F

Kiowa Indians {Kiowan}. 54-031-F, 54-134-F

Kitunahan Indians. See Kutenai Indians

Kiwai (Papuan people). 59-002-F, 83-899-F

Kiziba (African people). See Haya (African people)

Klahoquaht Indians. See Clayoquot Indians

Klallam Indians. See Clallam Indians

Klamath Indians. 54-033-F, 54-098-F, 54-133-F, 54-185-F

Klikitat Indians. 54-133-F, 57-014-F

Koetenay Indians. See Kutenai Indians

Kolanko. See Kuranko (African people)

Koluschan Indians. See Tlingit Indians

Kootenai Indians. See Kutenai Indians

Koranko. See Kuranko (African people)

Koreans. 83-899-F

Koryaks {Koriaks, Koriaques}. 54-149-F

Kota (Indic people). 54-080-F

Kuba (African people). 69-015-C

Kulaman. See Isneg

Kulanapan Indians. See Pomo Indians

Kuranko (African people) {Kulanko}. 54-003-F

Kutenai Indians. 57-014-F

Kwaaymi Indians. See Diegueño Indians

Kwakiutl Indians. 54-010-F, 54-035-F, 54-121-F, 57-014-F,
  83-917-F

Kwichan Indians. See Yuma Indians

Kwinaiult Indians. See Quinault Indians

Kwinti (Surinam people). See Djuka (Surinam people)

Ladinos (Spanish Jews). See Sephardim

Laguna Indians. 54-122-F

Lenape Indians {Lenni Lenape}. See Delaware Indians

Linapi. See Delaware Indians

Loma (African people). See Toma (African people)

Luba (African people). 69-015-C

Luiseño Indians. 54-123-F

Luvemba (African people). 59-002-F, 83-899-F

Macusi Indians {Macoushi, Macuchy, Macuxi}. 59-002-F,
  83-899-F

Mahampo (Philippine people). 54-079-F

Maidu Indians {Maideh}. 54-097-F

Moqui Indians. See Hopi Indians

Moslems. See Muslims

Mountaineer Indians. See Montagnais Indians

Muckaluck Indians. See Klamath Indians

Muskogee Indians {Muscogee, Muskoki}. See Creek Indians

Muslims. 59-002-F, 83-899-F

Nadowessioux Indians. See Dakota Indians

Nambé Indians. 54-135-F

Natchez Indians. 54-009-F

Native Americans (unidentified). See Indians of North
  America (unidentified)

Naudowessie Indians. See Dakota Indians

Navaho Indians {Navajo}. 54-039-F, 54-101-F, 54-118-F,
  54-125-F, 60-004-F

Nawdowissnee Indians. See Dakota Indians

Negroes (United States). See Afro-Americans

Nepalese. 54-076-F

Netlakapamuk Indians. See Ntlakyapamuk Indians

Netsiliks {Netsilingmiuts}. See Eskimos

Nez Percé Indians. 57-014-F

Ngangela (Bantu people). 59-002-F, 83-899-F

Ngoni. See Angoni

Nimapu {Nimipu}. See Nez Percé Indians

Nisqualli Indians. 54-131-F

Nitinat Indians. 54-041-F

Nooksack Indians {Nootsack}. 54-043-F

North American Indians (unidentified). See Indians of
  North America (unidentified)

Ntlakyapamuk Indians. 54-139-F, 59-002-F, 83-899-F

Numipu. See Nez Percé Indians

Nyamwezi. 59-002-F, 83-899-F

Nyanja (African people) {Nyasa}. 83-899-F

Ochipawa Indians. See Chippewa Indians

Oglala Indians {Ogallalla}. 54-112-F

Ojibwa Indians. See Chippewa Indians

Omaha Indians. 54-112-F, 54-140-F

Ona Indians. 59-002-F, 83-899-F

Oroches {Orochis}. 59-002-F, 83-899-F

Otchipwe Indians. See Chippewa Indians

Oto Indians {Otoe, Ottoe}. 54-140-F, 60-017-F

Ovimbundu (African people) {Ovimbali}. See Mbundu
  (African people)

Owyhees. See Hawaiians

Padlimiuts. See Eskimos

Paiute Indians {Pah-Ute}. 54-191-F, 60-017-F

Pakana'wo Indians. 54-134-F

Paloos Indians {Palouse, Palus}. 57-014-F

Pamunkey Indians. 60-018-F

Pangwa (Bantu people). See Wapangwa (Bantu people)

Pani Indians. See Pawnee Indians

Papago Indians. 54-042-F

Pawnee Indians. 54-011-F, 54-044-F, 54-045-F, 54-051-F,
  54-192-F, 59-002-F

Peigan Indians. See Piegan Indians

Pemon Indians. See Arecuna Indians

Penobscot Indians. 60-018-F

Pequea Indians. See Shawnee Indians

Permians {Permiaks, Permijaks, Permyaks}. 59-002-F,
  83-899-F

Piegan Indians. 54-096-F, 57-014-F

Pima Indians. 54-126-F, 54-228-F, 83-906-F

Pipatsje Indians. See Maricopa Indians

Piquaw Indians. See Shawnee Indians

Pit River Indians. See Achomawi Indians

Piute Indians. See Paiute Indians

Pomo Indians. 54-098-F

Ponca Indians {Ponka}. 54-140-F

Popo (African people). See Mina (African people)

Potawatomi Indians {Pottawatamie, Pottowatomie}. 54-140-F

Puerto Ricans. 54-148-F

Pujunan Indians. See Maidu Indians

Quechan Indians. See Yuma Indians

Quileute Indians {Quillayute, Quillehute}. 54-127-F,
  83-892-F

Quinault Indians {Quinaielt}. 54-128-F

Rechahecrian Indians. See Cherokee Indians

Red Indians of New Foundland. See Beothuk Indians

Ree Indians. See Arikara Indians

Ruandas (African people) {Ruandans}. 59-002-F, 83-899-F

Russians. 54-149-F

Rwandans. See Ruandas (African people)

Sa (African people). See Teke (African people)

Sahaptin Indians. See Nez Percé Indians

Salish Indians. 54-132-F, 57-014-F

Salteaux Indians. See Chippewa Indians

Samoans. 59-002-F, 83-899-F

Samoyeds. 59-002-F, 83-899-F

San Ildefonso Indians. 54-129-F

San Juan Indians. 54-134-F, 83-895-F

Sandawe. 59-002-F, 83-899-F

Santa Clara Indians. 54-135-F

Saquaqturmiuts. See Eskimos

Saramacca (Surinam people) {Saramaccaner, Saramaka}
   67-151-F

Sarsi Indians {Sarcee}. 54-136-F

Saulteaux Indians {Sauteux}. See Chippewa Indians

Scots. 83-922-C

Sefardic Jews. See Sephardim

Selknam Indians. See Ona Indians

Seneca Indians. 54-028-F

Sephardim {Sephardic Jews}. 59-002-F

Serrano Indians. 54-137-F

Shasta Indians. 54-185-F

Shawnee Indians {Shawanese, Shawanoe}. 54-107-F,
   54-141-F, 54-181-F, 60-017-F

Shoshoni Indians {Shoshone}. 54-185-F, 57-014-F, 60-017-F

Siamese. See Thais

Siksika Indians. 54-019-F, 54-094-C, 54-095-F, 54-096-F,
   64-040-F

Sindja (African people). See Zinza (African people)

Sinhalese {Singhalese}. 59-002-F, 83-899-F

Sioux Indians. See Dakota Indians

Skalzi Indians. See Kutenai Indians

Skittagetan Indians. See Haida Indians

Snake Indians. See Shoshoni Indians

Tsimshian Indians. 83-896-F

Tudas. See Todas

Tukubba (African people). See Kuba (African people)

Tunguses. 54-149-F

Tunica Indians. 54-009-F

Tunisians. 59-002-F

Tupirape Indians. See Tapirapé Indians

Turruba (African people). See Luba (African people)

Tusayan Indians. See Hopi Indians

Tuscarora Indians. 54-029-F

Tutelo Indians. 54-029-F

Twadux Indians {Tu-wa-dux Indians}. 57-014-F

Uchee Indians {Uchean}. See Yuchi Indians

Umbundu (African people). See Mbundu (African people)

Umea Indians. See Yuma Indians

Urhobo. See Sobo (African people)

Ute Indians {Uta}. 60-017-F

Uzigula. See Zigula (Bantu people)

Va Ngangela (Bantu people). See Ngangela (Bantu people)

Vakuanano (African people). See Mbundu (African people)

Valuga (African people) {Valugaluga Wanicha}. 59-002-F,
  83-899-F

Vandau (Bantu people). 54-065-F, 83-899-F

Veddahs {Vedda}. 59-002-F, 83-899-F

Wabanaki Indians. See Abnaki Indians

Wachaga (African people) {Wadschagga}. See Chaga (African
  people)

Wahaya (African people). See Haya (African people)

Index of Subjects

Agricultural songs
    Fon (African people): 67-152-F
    Huichol Indians: 59-002-F

Ancestor songs. See Songs for the dead

Animal imitations
    Caraja Indians: 54-053-F
    Nez Percé Indians: 57-014-F

Antelope
  dance songs
    Cochiti Indians: 54-106-F
    Paiute Indians: 54-191-F
  songs
    Hopi Indians: 54-027-F

Aguinaldos
    Puerto Ricans: 54-148-F

Art songs, French
    Unknown culture groups (Brazil): 54-053-F

Autumn songs
    Navaho Indians: 54-039-F
    Pawnee Indians: 54-044-F

Ballads
    Tibetans: 54-076-F

Ballets--Excerpts
    Americans: 80-086-C

Basket
  dance songs
    Unknown culture groups (New Mexico): 57-014-F

Boat songs
      Bakongo (African people):   54-210-F

Bombas
      Puerto Ricans: 54-148-F

Boys'
   dance songs
      Hopi Indians: 54-118-F
      San Juan Indians: 54-134-F
      Taos Indians: 54-138-F
   songs
      Bakongo (African people):   59-002-F, 83-899-F
      Kiowa Indians: 54-031-F

Bread dance songs
      Shawnee Indians: 54-181-F

Brothel songs
      Chinese: 54-150-F

Brush dance songs
      Hupa Indians: 54-120-F
      Yurok Indians: 54-098-F

Buffalo
   dance songs
      Acoma Indians: 54-101-F
      Cochiti Indians: 54-106-F, 83-919-F
      Creek Indians: 54-107-F
      Dakota Indians: 54-110-F
      Hidatsa Indians: 54-117-F
      Hopi Indians: 60-017-F
      Mandan Indians: 54-044-F, 54-117-F
      San Juan Indians: 54-134-F
      Shawnee Indians: 54-181-F
      Taos Indians: 54-138-F
      Unknown culture groups (New Mexico):   57-014-F
      Winnebago Indians: 54-140-F
      Zuñi Indians: 54-144-F
   songs
      Dakota Indians: 54-110-F, 54-112-F
      Hopi Indians: 54-027-F, 60-017-F
      Kiowa Indians: 54-031-F
      Pawnee Indians: 54-044-F, 54-045-F
      Salish Indians: 57-014-F
      Unknown culture groups (Montana):   57-014-F

Bull dance songs
      Piegan Indians: 54-096-F

Bundle songs.   See Medicine bundle songs

Butterfly dance songs
      Hopi Indians: 60-017-F
      San Juan Indians: 54-134-F

        Yorubas: 60-019-F

Decimas
        Puerto Ricans: 54-148-F

Deer
    dance songs
        Apache Indians: 54-103-F
        Cochiti Indians: 54-106-F
        Papago Indians: 54-042-F
        Piegan Indians: 54-096-F
        Taos Indians: 54-138-F
    songs
        Chehalis Indians: 54-131-F
        Eskimos: 54-115-F
        Kiowa Indians: 54-031-F
        Kutenai Indians: 57-014-F
        Yukian Indians: 54-098-F

Devils' songs
        Seneca Indians: 54-028-F

Dialogues
        Karadjeri (Australian people): 54-077-F

Doctors' songs
        Achomawi Indians: 54-013-F
        Arikara Indians: 54-044-F
        Chehalis Indians: 54-130-F, 54-131-F
        Cheyenne Indians: 54-104-F
        Clackamas Indians: 54-185-F
        Hupa Indians: 54-120-F
        Kalapuyan Indians: 54-185-F
        Kiowa Indians: 54-031-F
        Paiute Indians: 54-191-F
        Pawnee Indians: 54-045-F
        Pima Indians: 54-126-F
        Serrano Indians: 54-137-F
        Yukian Indians: 54-098-F

Dog
    dance songs
        San Juan Indians: 54-134-F
    songs
        Unknown culture groups (Montana): 57-014-F

Dream songs
        Dakota Indians: 54-110-F

Drinking
    dance songs
        Shawnee Indians: 54-181-F
    songs
        Arikara Indians: 54-044-F
        Chippewa Indians: 54-105-F
        Dakota Indians: 54-110-F

Farewell songs
    Samoans: 59-002-F, 83-899-F

Feast songs
    Cayuga Indians: 54-029-F
    Crow Indians: 54-108-F
    Dakota Indians: 54-110-F
    Klikitat Indians: 54-133-F
    Kwakiutl Indians: 54-035-F
    Papago Indians: 54-042-F
    Sarsi Indians: 54-136-F

Feather dance songs
    Chippewa Indians: 54-105-F
    Creek Indians: 54-107-F
    Seneca Indians: 54-028-F
    Yukian Indians: 54-098-F

Fertility dance songs
    Djuka (Surinam people): 67-151-F

Festival songs
    Acoma Indians: 54-101-F
    Dakota Indians: 54-112-F
    Diegueño Indians: 54-113-F
    Goajiro Indians: 54-054-F
    Luiseño Indians: 54-123-F
    Papago Indians: 54-042-F
    Puerto Ricans: 54-148-F
    Ruandas (African people): 59-002-F, 83-899-F
    Tagbanuas (Philippine people): 54-079-F

Fire
  dance songs
    Cayuga Indians: 54-029-F
    Tutelo Indians: 54-029-F
  power songs
    Clackamas Indians: 54-185-F

Fish dance songs
    Cayuga Indians: 54-029-F
    Creek Indians: 54-107-F
    Kwakiutl Indians: 54-035-F
    Seneca Indians: 54-028-F
    Unknown culture groups (Ontario): 54-029-F

Flower
  dance songs
    Hupa Indians: 54-120-F
    Taos Indians: 54-138-F
  songs
    Chinese: 54-150-F

Flute
  music
    Arhuaco Indians: 54-052-F

        Bagobo (Philippine people): 54-079-F
        Bamum (African people): 59-002-F, 83-899-F
        Bengalis: 54-076-F
        Chinese: 59-002-F, 83-899-F
        Desana Indians: 59-002-F, 83-899-F
        Diegueño Indians: 54-113-F
        Fon (African people): 67-152-F
        Goajiro Indians: 54-054-F
        Huichol Indians: 54-093-F
        Jamaicans: 54-147-F
        Kiowa Indians: 54-031-F
        Maricopa Indians: 54-228-F
        Mescalero Indians: 54-103-F
        Nepalese: 54-076-F
        Pawnee Indians: 54-051-F
        Pima Indians: 54-228-F
        Tunisians: 59-002-F
        Unknown culture groups (Philippines): 54-079-F
        Unknown culture groups (Sumatra): 59-002-F,
          83-899-F
        Unknown culture groups (Unknown locations):
          83-903-F
        Winnebago Indians: 54-140-F
        Yuchi Indians: 54-141-F
    songs
        Hopi Indians: 54-118-F
        Kiowa Indians: 54-031-F
        Pima Indians: 54-228-F, 83-906-F

Fog power songs
        Clackamas Indians: 54-185-F

Folk-songs
        Afro-Americans: 54-145-F, 83-911-F
        Americans: 75-199-C, 80-084-C, 83-890-F
        Koreans: 83-899-F

Folktales. See Stories, narratives and anecdotes

Fox
    dance songs
        Arikara Indians: 54-044-F
        Cheyenne Indians: 54-104-F
    songs
        Pawnee Indians: 54-045-F
        Unknown culture groups (Montana): 57-014-F
        Unknown culture groups (South Dakota): 57-014-F

Funeral rites and ceremonies
        Ashantis (African people): 67-152-F
        Bakongo (African people): 59-002-F, 83-899-F
        Diegueño Indians: 54-113-F
        Engganese (Indonesian people): 59-002-F, 83-899-F
        Fon (African people): 67-152-F
        Hopi Indians: 59-002-F, 83-899-F
        Jamaicans: 54-147-F

Karadjeri (Australian people): 54-077-F
Kiwai (Papuan people): 59-002-F, 83-899-F
Luiseño Indians: 54-123-F
Mandaya (Philippine people): 54-079-F
Saramacca (Surinam people): 67-151-F
Seneca Indians: 54-028-F
Serrano Indians: 54-137-F
Todas: 54-080-F
Wapangwa (Bantu people): 59-002-F, 83-899-F

Gambling songs
Chehalis Indians: 54-131-F
Cheyenne Indians: 54-104-F
Clackamas Indians: 54-185-F
Clallam Indians: 54-034-F
Cowlitz Indians: 54-133-F
Diegueño Indians: 54-113-F
Hupa Indians: 54-120-F
Klamath Indians: 54-098-F
Klikitat Indians: 57-014-F
Maidu Indians: 54-097-F
Nisqualli Indians: 54-131-F
Ntlakyapamuk Indians: 54-139-F
Paiute Indians: 60-017-F
Paloos Indians: 57-014-F
Salish Indians: 54-132-F
Sarsi Indians: 54-136-F
Twadux Indians: 57-014-F
Yakima Indians: 54-133-F
Zuñi Indians: 54-144-F

Game songs (unidentified)
Chehalis Indians: 54-130-F
Chinese: 54-150-F
Creek Indians: 54-107-F
Diegueño Indians: 54-114-F
Jamaicans: 54-147-F
Klamath Indians: 54-098-F
Kwakiutl Indians: 54-035-F
Maidu Indians: 54-097-F
Piegan Indians: 54-096-F
Pima Indians: 54-126-F
Puerto Ricans: 54-148-F
Ntlakyapamuk Indians: 59-002-F, 83-899-F
Sarsi Indians: 54-136-F
Serrano Indians: 54-137-F
Taos Indians: 54-138-F
Yuchi Indians: 54-141-F
Yuma Indians: 54-142-F
Zuñi Indians: 54-144-F

Gathering songs
Cowlitz Indians: 54-133-F
Klikitat Indians: 54-133-F
Taidnapam Indians: 54-133-F

Ghost
    dance songs
        Achomawi Indians: 54-013-F
        Cheyenne Indians: 54-104-F
        Dakota Indians: 54-110-F
        Hualapai Indians: 60-017-F
        Paiute Indians: 60-017-F
        Pawnee Indians: 54-044-F, 54-045-F, 59-002-F
        Shoshoni Indians: 57-014-F
    songs
        Cheyenne Indians: 54-104-F
        Kwakiutl Indians: 54-035-F
        Twadux Indians: 57-014-F

Gift distribution songs
        Taos Indians: 54-138-F

Girls'
    songs
        Papago Indians: 54-042-F
        Permians: 59-002-F, 83-899-F
    dance songs
        Cheyenne Indians: 54-104-F
        Hopi Indians: 54-118-F

Gospel music
        Afro-Americans: 54-145-F

Gourd dance songs
        Shawnee Indians: 54-181-F

Grass dance songs
        Assiniboin Indians: 54-017-F
        Atsina Indians: 57-014-F
        Dakota Indians: 54-110-F
        Piegan Indians: 54-096-F

Greeting songs
        Cheyenne Indians: 57-014-F
        Malecite Indians: 60-018-F
        Navaho Indians: 54-118-F
        Paiute Indians: 60-017-F
        Pawnee Indians: 54-044-F
        Penobscot Indians: 60-018-F
        Salish Indians: 57-014-F
        Saramacca (Surinam people): 67-151-F
        Unknown culture groups (United States): 83-896-F

Grinding songs
        Fon (African people): 67-152-F
        Hopi Indians: 54-118-F
        Laguna Indians: 54-122-F
        Marcusi Indians: 59-002-F, 83-899-F
        Navaho Indians: 54-118-F, 54-125-F
        Unknown culture groups (New Mexico): 57-014-F
        Zuñi Indians: 54-144-F

Guarachas
      Puerto Ricans: 54-148-F

Guessing game songs
      Winnebago Indians: 54-140-F

Hand
   dance songs
      Pawnee Indians: 54-044-F
   game songs
      Atsina Indians: 57-014-F
      Cheyenne Indians: 54-104-F
      Clackamas Indians: 54-185-F
      Kiowa Indians: 54-031-F
      Kutenai Indians: 57-014-F
      Molala Indians: 54-185-F
      Paiute Indians: 54-191-F
      Unknown culture groups (Montana):   57-014-F

Harvest dance songs
      Sanata Clara Indians: 54-135-F

Healing songs
      Arecuna Indians: 59-002-F, 83-899-F
      Arhuaco Indians: 54-052-F
      Bakongo (African people):   59-002-F, 83-899-F
      Batak (Palawan people):   54-079-F
      Cheyenne Indians: 54-104-F
      Cochiti Indians: 57-014-F
      Kiowa Indians: 54-031-F
      Klamath Indians: 54-033-F
      Kwakiutl Indians: 57-014-F
      Papago Indians: 54-042-F
      Pima Indians: 54-126-F
      Salish Indians: 57-014-F
      Seneca Indians: 54-028-F
      Unknown culture groups (Philippines):   54-079-F
      Wichita Indians: 54-031-F
      Yakima Indians: 57-014-F

Hiding
   dance songs
      Dakota Indians: 54-110-F
   game songs
      Dakota Indians: 54-110-F

Honoring songs. See Songs of honor and praise

Horse
   dance songs
      Creek Indians: 54-107-F
      Dakota Indians: 54-110-F, 54-112-F
      Yuchi Indians: 54-141-F
   songs
      Cheyenne Indians: 54-104-F

        Chinese: 54-150-F
        Dakota Indians: 54-112-F

Humorous songs
        Atsina Indians: 57-014-F
        British Americans: 54-140-F
        Clackamas Indians: 54-185-F
        Cowlitz Indians: 54-133-F
        Klikitat Indians: 54-133-F
        Malecite Indians: 60-018-F
        Penobscot Indians: 60-018-F
        San Juan Indians: 54-134-F
        Taidnapam Indians: 54-133-F
        Taos Indians: 54-138-F
        Unknown culture groups (Liberia): 54-003-F

Hunting
    dance songs
        Cochiti Indians: 54-106-F
    songs
        Acoma Indians: 54-101-F
        Apache Indians: 54-102-C, 54-103-F
        Ashantis (African people): 67-152-F
        British Americans: 54-095-F
        Creek Indians: 54-107-F
        Eskimos: 54-115-F
        Fon (African people): 67-152-F
        Hopi Indians: 54-027-F
        Kiowa Indians: 54-031-F
        Paiute Indians: 60-017-F
        Pima Indians: 54-126-F
        Siksika Indians: 54-094-F, 54-095-F
        Unknown culture groups (Northwest Territories):
            54-115-F
        Yorubas: 60-019-F
        Yukian Indians: 54-098-F

Hymns
        Acoma Indians: 54-101-F
        Eskimos: 54-115-F
        Huron Indians: 60-018-F
        Jamaicans: 54-147-F
        Malecite Indians: 60-018-F
        Mexicans: 54-101-F

Initiation rites
        Haida Indians: 57-014-F
        Nambé Indians: 54-135-F
        Zuñi Indians: 54-144-F

Instructional songs
        Luiseño Indians: 54-123-F

Instrumental music
        Americans: 75-199-C, 83-889-C, 83-902-C

Arhuaco Indians: 54-052-F
Balinese (Indonesian people): 59-002-F, 83-899-F
Bamum (African people): 59-002-F, 83-899-F
Bangi (African people): 69-015-F/C
Burmese: 59-002-F
Byelorussians: 59-002-F, 83-899-F
Chinese: 54-150-F, 59-002-F, 83-899-F
Diegueño Indians: 54-113-F
Fon (African people): 67-152-F
Gujaratis (Indic people): 59-002-F
Hausas: 59-002-F, 83-899-F
Haya (African people): 59-002-F, 83-899-F
Huichol Indians: 54-093-F
Jabo (African people): 54-223-F
Japanese: 59-002-F, 83-899-F
Javanese: 59-002-F
Kota (Indic people): 54-080-F
Kuba (African people): 69-015-F/C
Luba (African people): 69-015-F/C
Muslims: 59-002-F, 83-899-F
Puerto Ricans: 54-148-F
Russians: 54-149-F
Tagbanuas: 54-079-F
Thais: 59-002-F
Todas: 54-080-F
Unknown culture groups (Borneo): 59-002-F, 83-899-F
Unknown culture groups (Sumatra): 59-002-F,
   83-899-F
Unknown culture groups (Zaire): 69-015-F/C
Wamwera (African people): 83-899-F
Zigula (Bantu people): 59-002-F, 83-899-F

Invectives and derisions
Djuka (Surinam people): 67-151-F
Fon (African people): 67-152-F
Hopi Indians: 54-027-F
Ona Indians: 59-002-F, 83-899-F
Permians: 59-002-F, 83-899-F
Shawnee Indians: 54-181-F

Jigs
Americans: 75-199-C

Jumping dance songs
Hupa Indians: 54-120-F

Kachinas
Acoma Indians: 54-101-F, 57-014-F, 60-004-F
Hopi Indians: 54-027-F, 54-118-F, 54-119-F,
   60-017-F
Keresan Indians: 60-004-F
Laguna Indians: 54-122-F
Navaho Indians: 54-101-F, 54-118-F, 60-004-F
Zuñi Indians: 54-118-F, 54-144-F

Kick dance songs
      Hupa Indians: 54-120-F

Laments
      Africans: 54-065-F
      Ashantis (African people):   67-152-F
      Bakongo (African people):   59-002-F, 83-899-F
      Caraja Indians: 54-053-F
      Chinese: 54-150-F
      Clackamas Indians: 54-185-F
      Diegueño Indians: 54-114-F
      Ewe (African people):   59-002-F, 83-899-F
      Haida Indians: 57-014-F
      Kwakiutl Indians: 54-035-F
      Mandingo (African people):   54-003-F
      Paiute Indians: 60-017-F
      Serrano Indians: 54-137-F
      Shoshoni Indians: 60-017-F
      Tlingit Indians: 83-896-F
      Todas: 54-080-F
      Unknown culture groups (Papua New Guinea):
        59-002-F, 83-899-F
      Zulus: 54-065-F

Lightning songs
      Dakota Indians: 54-112-F
      Pawnee Indians: 54-044-F

Lodge songs
      Atsina Indians: 57-014-F
      Arapaho Indians: 57-014-F
      Cheyenne Indians: 54-104-F, 57-014-F
      Chippewa Indians: 54-105-F
      Crow Indians: 54-108-F
      Kiowa Indians: 54-031-F
      Kutenai Indians: 57-014-F
      Navaho Indians: 54-125-F
      Piegan Indians: 54-096-F, 57-014-F
      Siksika Indians: 54-095-F
      Wishram Indians: 57-014-F
      Unknown culture groups (Montana):   57-014-F
      Unknown culture groups (Washington State):   57-014-F

Loon songs
      Achomawi Indians: 54-013-F

Love songs
      Arapaho Indians: 57-014-F
      Arhuaco Indians: 54-052-F
      Assiniboin Indians: 54-017-F
      Ashantis (African people):   67-152-F
      Chehalis Indians: 54-130-F, 54-131-F
      Cheyenne Indians: 54-104-F, 57-014-F
      Chinese: 54-150-F
      Chinook Indians: 54-133-F

Lullabies
        Atsina Indians: 57-014-F
        Chehalis Indians: 54-130-F, 54-131-F
        Clackamas Indians: 54-185-F
        Cowlitz Indians: 54-133-F
        Fon (African people): 67-152-F
        Hesquiat Indians: 57-014-F
        Hopi Indians: 54-027-F, 54-118-F
        Indians of North America (unidentified): 83-893-F
        Kwakiutl Indians: 54-035-F
        Montagnais Indians: 60-018-F
        Pamunkey Indians: 60-018-F
        Penobscot Indians: 60-018-F
        Pima Indians: 54-126-F
        Serrano Indians: 54-137-F
        Shawnee Indians: 54-181-F
        Taidnapam Indians: 54-133-F
        Unknown culture groups (Papua New Guinea):
          59-002-F, 83-899-F
        Yorubas: 60-019-F

Malagueñas
        Puerto Ricans: 54-148-F

Marches
        Americans: 75-199-C, 83-889-C

Marriage rites and ceremonies
        Chehalis Indians: 54-131-F
        Chinese: 54-150-F
        Fon (African people): 67-152-F
        Hopi Indians: 54-027-F
        Huron Indians: 60-018-F
        Nepalese: 54-076-F
        Penobscot Indians: 60-018-F
        Russians: 54-149-F
        Seneca Indians: 54-028-F
        Unknown culture groups (New Mexico): 57-014-F
        Unknown culture groups (United States): 60-018-F

Mask songs
        Acoma Indians: 57-014-F
        Haida Indians: 57-014-F
        Kwakiutl Indians: 57-014-F

Mazurkas
        Puerto Ricans: 54-148-F

Medicine
    bundle songs
        Arikara Indians: 54-044-F
        Kainah Indians: 54-096-F
        Pawnee Indians: 54-044-F, 54-192-F
        Piegan Indians: 54-096-F, 57-014-F

        Ntlakyapamuk Indians: 54-139-F
        Pawnee Indians: 54-044-F

Mescal songs
        Winnebago Indians: 54-140-F

Mocassin
    dance songs
        Chippewa Indians: 54-105-F
        Shawnee Indians: 54-181-F
    game songs
        Chippewa Indians: 54-105-F
    songs
        Winnebago Indians: 54-140-F

Moon songs
        Chehalis Indians: 54-131-F
        Kainah Indians: 54-096-F

Morning songs
        Kiowa Indians: 54-031-F
        Kwakiutl Indians: 57-014-F
        Todas: 54-080-F

Mothers' songs
        Kiowa Indians: 54-031-F

Mourning songs. See Laments

Mouse power songs
        Clackamas Indians: 54-185-F

Music, Popular
        Americans: 54-041-F, 75-199-C, 80-084-C, 80-085-C,
          80-086-C, 83-889-C, 83-902-C, 83-922-C
        Chinese: 54-150-F
        Germans: 75-199-C
        Nitinat Indians: 54-041-F
        Scots: 83-922-C
        Unknown culture groups (Philippines): 54-079-F

Musical intervals and scales
        Pawnee Indians: 54-051-F

Myth songs
        Chehalis Indians: 54-131-F
        Cowlitz Indians: 54-133-F
        Klikitat Indians: 54-133-F
        Maricopa Indians: 54-228-F
        Nisqualli Indians: 54-131-F
        Pima Indians: 54-126-F, 54-228-F

Mythology
        Chehalis Indians: 54-130-F, 54-131-F
        Clackamas Indians: 54-185-F
        Malecite Indians: 60-018-F

Personal songs
        Clackamas Indians: 54-185-F
        Cowlitz Indians: 54-133-F
        Fon (African people):   67-152-F
        Hopi Indians: 54-027-F
        Klikitat Indians: 54-133-F
        Kota (Indic people):   54-080-F
        San Juan Indians: 54-134-F
        Taidnapam Indians: 54-133-F

Peyote songs
        Cheyenne Indians: 60-017-F
        Dakota Indians: 54-110-F
        Kickapoo Indians: 60-017-F
        Kiowa Indians: 54-031-F
        Pawnee Indians: 54-044-F, 54-045-F
        Shawnee Indians: 54-181-F

Pigeon dance songs
        Cayuga Indians: 54-029-F

Pipe
    dance songs
        Pawnee Indians: 54-044-F
    songs
        Atsina Indians: 57-014-F
        Kiowa Indians: 54-031-F
        Piegan Indians: 54-096-F
        Sarsi Indians: 54-136-F

Planting songs
        Bakongo (African people):   59-002-F, 83-899-F
        Cayuga Indians: 54-029-F
        Delaware Indians: 54-029-F
        Papago Indians: 54-042-F
        Tutelo Indians: 54-029-F
        Unknown culture groups (Ontario):   54-029-F

Polkas
        Americans: 83-889-C
        Jamaicans: 54-147-F
        Puerto Ricans: 54-148-F

Potlatch songs
        Cowichan Indians: 57-014-F
        Kwakiutl Indians: 54-010-F, 54-035-F
        Ntlakyapamuk Indians: 54-139-F
        Unknown culture groups (United States or Canada):
            57-014-F

Power songs (unidentified)
        Clackamas Indians: 54-185-F
        Kalapuyan Indians: 54-185-F
        Molala Indians: 54-185-F

Powwow songs.   See Meeting songs